Agnes Calder Smith
5, Rustic Place
Dundee

The Country of the Pointed Firs

'Flexibles'

Uniform with this book

The Story of the Jews by Louis Browne
Selections from Byron edited by Hamish Miles
December the Fourteenth by Dmitri Merezhkovsky
Men Without Women by Ernest Hemingway
A Portrait of the Artist as a Young Man by James Joyce
Dubliners (Stories) by James Joyce
Twenty-five (an Autobiography) by Beverley Nichols
Mastro-Don Gesualdo by Giovanni Verga. *With an Introduction by D. H. Lawrence*
Italian Backgrounds by Edith Wharton

The Country of the Pointed Firs

Sarah Orne Jewett

Jonathan Cape
Thirty Bedford Square
London

First published 1927
First issued in *Flexibles* 1934

JONATHAN CAPE LTD. 30 BEDFORD SQUARE, LONDON
AND 91 WELLINGTON STREET WEST, TORONTO

PRINTED IN GREAT BRITAIN BY
THE GARDEN CITY PRESS LTD., LETCHWORTH, HERTS.
PAPER BY JOHN DICKINSON & CO. LTD.
BOUND BY A. W. BAIN & CO. LTD. IN CLOTH,
FAST TO LIGHT AND WASHABLE, MADE BY
MORTON SUNDOUR FABRICS LTD.

CONTENTS

PREFACE

But give to thine own story
Simplicity, with glory.

LOUISE IMOGEN GUINEY

IN reading over a package of letters from Sarah Orne Jewett, I find this observation: '*The thing that teases the mind over and over for years, and at last gets itself put down rightly on paper—whether little or great, it belongs to Literature.*' Miss Jewett was very conscious of the fact that when a writer makes anything that belongs to Literature (limiting the term here to imaginative literature, which she of course meant), his material goes through a process very different from that by which he makes merely a good story or a good novel. No one can exactly define this process; but certainly persistence, survival, recurrence in the writer's mind, are highly characteristic of it. The shapes and scenes that have 'teased' the mind for years, when they do at last get themselves rightly put down, make a very much higher order of writing, and a much more costly, than the most vivid and vigorous transfer of immediate impressions.

In some of Miss Jewett's earlier books, *Deephaven, Country Byways, Old Friends and New*, one can find first sketches, first impressions, which later crystallised into the almost flawless examples of literary art that make up this volume. One can, as it were, watch

7

in process the two kinds of making: the first, which is full of perception and feeling but rather fluid and formless, the second, which is so tightly built and significant in design. The design is, indeed, so happy, so right, that it seems inevitable; the design is the story and the story is the design. These sketches are living things caught in the open, with light and freedom and air-spaces about them. They melt into the land and the life of the land until they are not stories at all, but life itself.

A great many good stories were being written upon New England themes at the same time that Miss Jewett was writing; stories that to many contemporary readers may have seemed more interesting than hers, because they dealt with more startling 'situations,' were more heavily accented, more elaborately costumed and posed in the studio. But most of them are not very interesting to read and re-read to-day; they have not the one thing that survives all arresting situations, all good writing and clever story making – inherent individual beauty; the kind of beauty we feel when a beautiful song is sung by a beautiful voice that is exactly suited to the song.

Pater said that every truly great drama must, in the end, linger in the reader's mind as a sort of ballad. Probably the same thing might be said of every great story. It must leave in the mind of the sensitive reader an intangible residuum of pleasure; a cadence, a quality of voice that is exclusively the writer's own, individual, unique. A quality that one can remember without the volume at hand, can experience over and over again in the mind but can never absolutely define, as one can experience in memory a melody, or the summer perfume of a garden. The magnitude of the subject-matter is not of primary importance, seemingly. An idyl of Theocritus, concerned with sheep and goats and shade and pastures, is to-day as much alive as the most dramatic passages of the Iliad – stirs the reader's feeling quite as much, perhaps, if the reader is a poet.

It is a common fallacy that a writer, if he is talented enough, can achieve this poignant quality by improving upon his subject-matter, by using his 'imagination' upon it and twisting it to suit his purpose. The truth is that by such a process (which is not imaginative at all!) he can at best produce only a brilliant sham, which, like a badly built and pretentious house, looks poor and shabby in a few years. If he achieves anything noble, anything enduring, it must be by giving himself absolutely to his material. And this gift of sympathy is his great gift ; is the fine thing in him that alone can make his work fine. He fades away into the land and people of his heart, he dies of love only to be born again. The artist spends a life-time in loving the things that haunt him, in having his mind 'teased' by them, in trying to get these conceptions down on paper exactly as they are to him and not in conventional poses supposed to reveal their character; trying this method and that, as a painter tries different lightings and different attitudes with his

subject to catch the one that presents it more sugges-
tively than any other. And at the end of a lifetime he
emerges with much that is more or less happy experi-
menting, and comparatively little that is the very flower
of himself and his genius. I have tried to gather into
this volume the very best of Miss Jewett's beautiful
work; the stories which, read by an eager student fifty
years from now, will give him the characteristic flavour,
the spirit, the cadence, of an American writer of the
first order – and of a New England which will then be
a thing of the past.

The stories chosen for this volume vary little in
quality, though one may have one's favourites among
them. The story *William's Wedding* was uncom-
pleted at the time of Miss Jewett's death, and while all
the essentials of the picture are there, the writing is in
places a little vague, lacks the last co-ordinating touch
of the writer's hand.

To note an artist's limitations is but to define his
genius. A reporter can write equally well about
everything that is presented to his view, but a creative
writer can do his best only with what lies within the
range and character of his talent. These stories of
Miss Jewett's have much to do with fisher-folk and
seaside villages; with juniper pastures and lonely farms,
neat grey country houses and delightful, well-seasoned
old men and women. That, when one thinks of it in a
flash, is New England. I remember hearing an English
actor say that until he made a motor trip through New

England he had supposed that the Americans killed their aged in some merciful fashion, for he saw none in the cities where he played.

There are many kinds of people in the State of Maine, and its neighbouring States, who are not in Miss Jewett's books. There may be Othellos and Iagos and Don Juans, but they are not highly characteristic of the country, they do not come up spontaneously in the juniper pastures as the everlasting does. Miss Jewett wrote of the people who grew out of the soil and the life of the country near her heart, not about exceptional individuals at war with their environment. This was not a creed with her, but an instinctive preference. She once laughingly told me that her head was full of dear old houses and dear old women, and that when an old house and an old woman came together in her brain with a click, she knew that a story was under way.

Born within the scent of the sea but not within sight of it, in a beautiful old house full of strange and lovely things brought home from all over the globe by sea-faring ancestors, she spent much of her girlhood driving about the country with her doctor father on his professional rounds among the farms. She early learned to love her country for what it was. What is quite as important, she saw it as it was. She happened to have the right nature, the right temperament, to see it so — and to understand by intuition the deeper meaning of all she saw.

She had not only the eye, she had the ear. From childhood she must have treasured up those pithy bits of local speech, of native idiom, which enrich and enliven her pages. The language her people speak to each other is a native tongue. No writer can invent it. It is made in the hard school of experience, in communities where language has been undisturbed long enough to take on colour and character from the nature and experiences of the people. The 'sayings' of a community, its proverbs, are its characteristic comment upon life; they imply its history, suggest its attitude toward the world, and its way of accepting life. Such an idiom makes the finest language any writer can have; and he can never get it with a notebook. He himself must be able to think and feel in that speech – it is a gift from heart to heart.

Much of Miss Jewett's delightful humour comes from her delicate and tactful handling of this native language of the waterside and countryside, never overdone, never pushed a shade too far; from this, and from her own fine attitude toward her subject-matter. This attitude in itself, though unspoken, is everywhere felt, and constitutes one of the most potent elements of grace and charm in her stories. She had with her own stories and her own characters a very charming relation; spirited, gay, tactful, noble in its essence and a little arch in its expression. In this particular relationship many of our most gifted writers are unfortunate. If a writer's attitude toward his characters and his scene is as vulgar as a showman's, as mercenary as an auctioneer's, vulgar and meretricious will his product remain forever.

Gilbert Murray has illustrated the two kinds of beauty in writing by a happy similitude. There is a kind of beauty, he says, which comes from rich ornamentation; like the splendour one might admire on a Chinese junk, gorgeously gilded and painted, hung with rich embroideries and tapestries. Then there is the beauty of a modern yacht, where there is no ornamentation at all; our whole sensation of pleasure in watching a yacht under sail comes from the fact that every line of the craft is designed for one purpose, that everything about it furthers that purpose, so that it has an organic, living simplicity and directness. This, he says, is the beauty for which the Greek writers strove; it is certainly that for which Miss Jewett strove.

If I were asked to name three American books which have the possibility of a long, long life, I would say at once, *The Scarlet Letter, Huckleberry Finn,* and *The Country of the Pointed Firs.* I can think of no others that confront time and change so serenely. The latter book seems to me fairly to shine with the reflection of its long, joyous future. It is so tightly yet so lightly built, so little encumbered with heavy materialism that deteriorates and grows old-fashioned. I like to think with what pleasure, with what a sense of rich discovery, the young student of American literature in far distant years to come will take up this book and say, 'A masterpiece!' as proudly as if he himself had made it. It will be a message to the future, a message in a universal language, like the tuft of meadow flowers in Robert Frost's fine poem, which the mower abroad in the early morning left standing, just skirted by the scythe, for the mower of the afternoon to gaze upon and wonder at – the one message that even the scythe of Time spares.

WILLA CATHER

. . . *I always think of her as of one who, hearing New England accused of being a bleak land without beauty, passes confidently over the snow, and by the grey rock, and past the dark fir tree, to a southern bank, and there, brushing away the decayed leaves, triumphantly shows to the fault-finder a spray of the trailing arbutus. And I should like, for my own part, to add this: that the fragrant, retiring, exquisite flower, which I think she would say is the symbol of New England virtue, is the symbol also of her own modest and delightful art.*

From THE ART OF MISS JEWETT, by Charles Miner Thompson, in the *Atlantic* for October, 1904.

CHAPTER ONE

The Return

*

THERE was something about the coast town of Dunnet which made it seem more attractive than other maritime villages of eastern Maine. Perhaps it was the simple fact of acquaintance with that neighbourhood which made it so attaching, and gave such interest to the rocky shore and dark woods, and the few houses which seemed to be securely wedged and tree-nailed in among the ledges by the Landing. These houses made the most of their seaward view, and there was a gaiety and determined floweriness in their bits of garden ground; the small-paned high windows in the peaks of their steep gables were like knowing eyes that watched the harbour and the far sea-line beyond, or looked north-ward all along the shore and its background of spruces and balsam firs. When one really knows a village like this and its surroundings, it is like becoming acquainted with a single person. The process of falling in love at first sight is as final as it is swift in such a case, but the growth of true friendship may be a life-long affair.

After a first brief visit made two or three summers before in the course of a yachting cruise, a lover of Dunnet Landing returned to find the unchanged shores of the pointed firs, the same quaintness of the village with its elaborate conventionalities; all that mixture of remoteness, and childish certainty of being the centre of civilisation of which her affectionate dreams had told. One evening in June, a single passenger landed upon the steamboat wharf. The tide was high, there was a fine crowd of spectators, and the younger portion of the company followed her with subdued excitement up the narrow street of the salt-aired, white-clap-boarded little town·

CHAPTER TWO

Mrs. Todd

LATER, there was only one fault to find with this
choice of a summer lodging-place, and that was its
complete lack of seclusion. At first the tiny house of
Mrs. Almira Todd, which stood with its end to the
street, appeared to be retired and sheltered enough
from the busy world, behind its bushy bit of a green
garden, in which all the blooming things, two or
three gay hollyhocks and some London-pride,
were pushed back against the grey-shingled wall.
It was a queer little garden and puzzling to a
stranger, the few flowers being put at a disadvantage
by so much greenery; but the discovery was soon
made that Mrs. Todd was an ardent lover of herbs,
both wild and tame, and the sea-breezes blew into
the low end-window of the house laden with not
only sweet-brier and sweet-mary, but balm and sage
and borage and mint, wormwood and southernwood.
If Mrs. Todd had occasion to step into the far corner
of her herb plot, she trod heavily upon thyme, and
made its fragrant presence known with all the rest.
Being a very large person, her full skirts brushed
and bent almost every slender stalk that her feet
missed. You could always tell when she was stepping
about there, even when you were half awake in the
morning, and learned to know, in the course of a few

weeks' experience, in exactly which corner of the garden she might be.

At one side of this herb plot were other growths of a rustic pharmacopœia, great treasures and rarities among the commoner herbs. There were some strange and pungent odours that roused a dim sense and remembrance of something in the forgotten past. Some of these might once have belonged to sacred and mystic rites, and have had some occult knowledge handed with them down the centuries; but now they pertained only to humble compounds brewed at intervals with molasses or vinegar or spirits in a small caldron on Mrs. Todd's kitchen stove. They were dispensed to suffering neighbours, who usually came at night as if by stealth, bringing their own ancient-looking vials to be filled. One nostrum was called the Indian remedy, and its price was but fifteen cents; the whispered directions could be heard as customers passed the windows. With most remedies the purchaser was allowed to depart unadmonished from the kitchen, Mrs. Todd being a wise saver of steps; but with certain vials she gave cautions, standing in the doorway, and there were other doses which had to be accompanied on their healing way as far as the gate, while she muttered long chapters of directions, and kept up an air of secrecy and importance to the last. It may not have been only the common ails of humanity with which she tried to cope; it seemed sometimes as if love and hate and jealousy and adverse winds at sea might also find their proper remedies among the curious wild-looking plants in Mrs. Todd's garden.

The village doctor and this learned herbalist were upon the best of terms. The good man may have counted upon the unfavourable effect of certain potions which he should find his opportunity in counteracting; at any rate, he now and then stopped and exchanged greetings with Mrs. Todd over the picket fence. The conversation became at once professional after the briefest preliminaries, and he would stand twirling a sweet-scented sprig in his fingers, and make suggestive jokes, perhaps about her faith in a too persistent course of thoroughwort elixir, in which my landlady professed such firm belief as sometimes to endanger the life and usefulness of worthy neighbours.

To arrive at this quietest of seaside villages late in June, when the busy herb-gathering season was just beginning, was also to arrive in the early prime of Mrs. Todd's activity in the brewing of old-fashioned spruce beer. This cooling and refreshing drink had been brought to wonderful perfection through a long series of experiments; it had won immense local fame, and the supplies for its manufacture were always giving out and having to be replenished. For various reasons, the seclusion and uninterrupted days which had been looked forward to proved to be very rare in this otherwise delightful corner of the world. My hostess and I had made our shrewd business agreement on the basis of a simple cold luncheon at noon, and liberal restitution in the matter of hot suppers, to provide for which the lodger might sometimes be seen hurrying down the road, late in the day, with cunner line in hand. It was soon found that this arrangement made large allowance for Mrs. Todd's slow herb-gathering progresses through woods and pastures. The spruce-beer customers were pretty steady in hot weather, and there were many demands for different soothing syrups and elixirs with which the unwise curiosity of my early residence had made me acquainted. Knowing Mrs. Todd to be a widow, who had little beside this slender business and the income from one hungry lodger to maintain her, one's energies and even interest were quickly bestowed, until it became a matter of course that she should go afield every pleasant day, and that the lodger should answer all peremptory knocks at the side door.

In taking an occasional wisdom-giving stroll in Mrs. Todd's company, and in acting as business partner during her frequent absences, I found the July days fly fast, and it was not until I felt myself confronted with too great pride and pleasure in the display, one night, of two dollars and twenty-seven cents which I had taken in during the day, that I remembered a long piece of writing, sadly belated now, which I was bound to do. To have been patted kindly on the shoulder and called 'darlin',' to have been offered a surprise of early mushrooms for supper, to have had all the glory of making two dollars and twenty-seven cents in a single day, and

then to renounce it all and withdraw from these pleasant
successes, needed much resolution. Literary employ-
ments are so vexed with uncertainties at best, and it was
not until the voice of conscience sounded louder in my
ears than the sea on the nearest pebble beach that I
said unkind words of withdrawal to Mrs. Todd. She
only became more wistfully affectionate than ever in
her expressions, and looked as disappointed as I expected when I frankly told her that I could no longer
enjoy the pleasure of what we called 'seein' folks.' I
felt that I was cruel to a whole neighbourhood in cur-
tailing her liberty in this most important season for
harvesting the different wild herbs that were so much
counted upon to ease their winter ails.

'Well, dear,' she said sorrowfully, 'I've took great
advantage o' your bein' here. I ain't had such a season
for years, but I have never had nobody I could so trust.
All you lack is a few qualities, but with time you'd
gain judgment an' experience, an' be very able in the
business. I'd stand right here an' say it to anybody.'

Mrs. Todd and I were not separated or estranged by
the change in our business relations; on the contrary, a
deeper intimacy seemed to begin. I do not know what
herb of the night it was that used sometimes to send
out a penetrating odour late in the evening, after the
dew had fallen, and the moon was high, and the cool
air came up from the sea. Then Mrs. Todd would feel
that she must talk to somebody, and I was only too glad

to listen. We both fell under the spell, and she either stood outside the window, or made an errand to my sitting-room, and told, it might be very commonplace news of the day, or, as happened one misty summer night, all that lay deepest in her heart. It was in this way that I came to know that she had loved one who was far above her.

'No, dear, him I speak of could never think of me,' she said. 'When we was young together his mother didn't favour the match, an' done everything she could to part us; and folks thought we both married well, but 'twa'n't what either one of us wanted most; an' now we're left alone again, an' might have had each other all the time. He was above bein' a seafarin' man, an' prospered more than most; he come of a high family, an' my lot was plain an' hard-workin'. I ain't seen him for some years; he's forgot out youthful feelin's, I expect, but a woman's heart is different; them feelin's comes back when you think you've done with 'em, as sure as spring comes with the year. An' I've always had ways of hearin' about him.'

She stood in the centre of a braided rug, and its rings of black and gray seemed to circle about her feet in the dim light. Her height and massiveness in the low room gave her the look of a huge sibyl, while the strange fragrance of the mysterious herb blew in from the little garden.

CHAPTER THREE

The Schoolhouse

✿

FOR some days after this, Mrs. Todd's customers came and went past my windows, and, haying-time being nearly over, strangers began to arrive from the inland country, such was her widespread reputation. Sometimes I saw a pale young creature like a white wind-flower left over into midsummer, upon whose face consumption had set its bright and wistful mark; but oftener two stout, hard-worked women from the farms came together, and detailed their symptoms to Mrs. Todd in loud and cheerful voices, combining the satisfactions of a friendly gossip with the medical opportunity. They seemed to give much from their own store of therapeutic learning. I became aware of the school in which my landlady had strengthened her natural gift; but hers was always the governing mind, and the final command, 'Take of hy'sop one handful' (or whatever herb it was), was received in respectful silence. One afternoon, when I had listened, it was impossible not to listen, with cottonless ears, and then laughed and listened again, with an idle pen in my hand, during a particularly spirited and personal conversation, I reached for my hat, and, taking blotting-book and all under my arm, I resolutely fled further temptation, and walked out past the fragrant green garden and up the dusty road. The way went straight uphill, and presently I stopped and turned to look back.

The tide was in, the wide harbour was surrounded by its dark woods, and the small wooden houses stood as near as they could get to the landing. Mrs. Todd's was the last house on the way inland. The gray ledges of the rocky shore were well covered with sod in most places, and the pasture bayberry and wild roses grew thick among them. I could see the higher inland country and the scattered farms. On the brink of the hill stood a little white schoolhouse, much wind-blown and weather-beaten, which was a landmark to seagoing folk; from its door there was a most beautiful view of sea and shore. The summer vacation now prevailed, and after finding the door unfastened, and taking a long look through one of the seaward windows, and reflecting afterward for some time in a shady place near by among the bayberry bushes, I returned to the chief place of business in the village, and, to the amusement of two of the select-men, brothers and autocrats of Dunnet Landing, I hired the schoolhouse for the rest of the vacation for fifty cents a week.

Selfish as it may appear, the retired situation seemed to possess great advantages, and I spent many days there quite undisturbed, with the sea-breeze blowing through the small, high windows and swaying the heavy outside shutters to and fro. I hung my hat and luncheon-basket on an entry nail as if I were a small scholar, but I sat at the teacher's desk as if I were that great authority, with all the timid empty benches in rows before me. Now and then an idle sheep came and stood for a long time looking in at the door. At sundown I went back, feeling most businesslike, down toward the village again, and usually met the flavour not of the herb garden, but of Mrs. Todd's hot supper, halfway up the hill. On the nights when there were evening meetings or other public exercises that demanded her presence we had tea very early, and I was welcomed back as if from a long absence.

Once or twice I feigned excuses for staying at home, while Mrs. Todd made distant excursions, and came home late, with both hands full and a heavily laden apron. This was in pennyroyal time, and when the rare lobelia was in its prime and the elecampane was coming on. One day she appeared at the schoolhouse itself, partly out of amused curiosity about my industries; but she explained that there was no tansy in the neighbourhood with such snap to it as some that grew about the schoolhouse lot. Being scuffed down all the spring made it grow so much the better, like some folks that had it hard in their youth, and were bound to make the most of themselves before they died.

CHAPTER FOUR

At the Schoolhouse Window

★

ONE day I reached the schoolhouse very late, owing to attendance upon the funeral of an acquaintance and neighbour, with whose sad decline in health I had been familiar, and whose last days both the doctor and Mrs. Todd had tried in vain to ease. The services had taken place at one o'clock, and now, at quarter past two, I stood at the schoolhouse window, looking down at the procession as it went along the lower road close to the shore. It was a walking funeral, and even at that distance I could recognise most of the mourners as they went their solemn way. Mrs. Begg had been very much respected, and there was a large company of friends following to her grave. She had been brought up on one of the neighbouring farms, and each of the few times that I had seen her she professed great dissatisfaction with town life. The people lived too close together for her liking, at the Landing, and she could not get used to the constant sound of the sea. She had lived to lament three seafaring husbands, and her house was decorated with West Indian curiosities, specimens of conch shells and fine coral which they had brought home from their voyages in lumber-laden ships. Mrs. Todd had told me all our neighbour's history. They had been girls together, and, to use her own phrase, had 'both seen trouble till they knew the best and worst on't.'

I could see the sorrowful, large figure of Mrs. Todd as I stood at the window. She made a break in the procession by walking slowly and keeping the after-part of it back. She held a handkerchief to her eyes, and I knew with a pang of sympathy, that hers was not affected grief.

Beside her, after much difficulty, I recognised the one strange and unrelated person in all the company, an old man who had always been mysterious to me. I could see his thin, bending figure. He wore a narrow, long-tailed coat and walked with a stick, and had the same 'cant to leeward' as the wind-bent trees on the height above.

This was Captain Littlepage, whom I had seen only once or twice before, sitting pale and old behind a closed window; never out of doors until now. Mrs. Todd always shook her head gravely when I asked a question, and said that he wasn't what he had been once, and seemed to class him with her other secrets. He might have belonged with a simple which grew in a certain slug-haunted corner of the garden, whose use she could never be betrayed into telling me, though I saw her cutting the tops by moonlight once, as if it were a charm, and not a medicine, like the great fading bloodroot leaves.

I could see that she was trying to keep pace with the old captain's lighter steps. He looked like an aged grasshopper of some strange human variety. Behind this pair was a short, impatient, little person, who kept the captain's house, and gave it what Mrs. Todd and others believed to be no proper sort of care. She was usually called 'that Mari' Harris' in subdued conversation between intimates, but they treated her with anxious civility when they met her face to face.

The bay-sheltered islands and the great sea beyond stretched away to the far horizon southward and eastward; the little procession in the foreground looked futile and helpless on the edge of the rocky shore. It was a glorious day early in July, with a clear, high sky; there were no clouds, there was no noise of the sea. The song sparrows sang and sang, as if with joyous knowledge of immortality, and contempt for those who could so pettily concern themselves with death. I stood watching until the funeral procession had crept round a shoulder of the slope below and disappeared from the great landscape as if it had gone into a cave.

An hour later I was busy at my work. Now and then a bee blundered in and took me for an enemy; but there was a useful stick upon the teacher's desk, and I rapped to call the bees to order as if they were unruly scholars, or waved them away from their riots over the ink, which I had bought at the Landing store, and discovered too late to be scented with bergamot, as if to refresh the labours of anxious scribes. One anxious scribe felt very dull that day; a sheep-bell tinkled near by, and called her wandering wits after it. The sentences failed to catch these lovely summer cadences. For the first time I began to wish for a companion and for news from the outer world, which had been, half-unconsciously, forgotten. Watching the funeral gave one a sort of pain. I began to wonder if I ought not to have walked with the rest, instead of hurrying away at the end of the services. Perhaps the Sunday gown I had put on for the occasion was making this disastrous change of feeling, but I had now made myself and my friends remember that I did not really belong to Dunnet Landing.

I sighed, and turned to the half-written page again.

CHAPTER FIVE

Captain Littlepage

★

IT was a long time after this; an hour was very long in that coast town where nothing stole away the shortest minute. I had lost myself completely in work, when I heard footsteps outside. There was a steep footpath between the upper and the lower road, which I climbed to shorten the way, as the children had taught me, but I believed that Mrs. Todd would find it inaccessible, unless she had occasion to seek me in great haste. I wrote on, feeling like a besieged miser of time, while the footsteps came nearer, and the sheep-bell tinkled away in haste as if someone had shaken a stick in its wearer's face. Then I looked and saw Captain Littlepage passing the nearest window; the next moment he tapped politely at the door.

'Come in, sir,' I said, rising to meet him; and he entered, bowing with much courtesy. I stepped down from the desk and offered him a chair by the window, where he seated himself at once, being sadly spent by his climb. I returned to my fixed seat behind the teacher's desk, which gave him the lower place of a scholar.

'You ought to have the place of honour, Captain Littlepage,' I said.

'A happy, rural seat of various views,' he quoted, as he gazed out into the sunshine and up the long, wooded shore. Then he glanced at me, and looked all about him as pleased as a child.

'My quotation was from Paradise Lost: the greatest of poems, I suppose you know?' and I nodded. 'There's nothing that ranks, to my mind, with Paradise Lost; it's all lofty, all lofty,' he continued. 'Shakespeare was a great poet; he copied life, but you have to put up with a great deal of low talk.'

I now remembered that Mrs. Todd had told me one day that Captain Littlepage had overset his mind with too much reading; she had also made dark reference to his having 'spells' of some unexplainable nature. I could not help wondering what errand had brought him out in search of me. There was something quite charming in his appearance: it was a face thin and delicate with refinement, but worn into appealing lines, as if he had suffered from loneliness and misapprehension. He looked, with his careful precision of dress, as if he were the object of cherishing care on the part of elderly unmarried sisters, but I knew Mari' Harris to be a very commonplace, inelegant person, who would have no such standards; it was plain that the captain was his own attentive valet. He sat looking at me expectantly. I could not help thinking that, with his queer head and length of thinness, he was made to hop along the road of life rather than to walk. The captain was very grave indeed, and I bade my inward spirit keep close to discretion.

'Poor Mrs. Begg has gone,' I ventured to say.

I still wore my Sunday gown by way of showing respect.

'She has gone,' said the captain, – 'very easy at the last, I was informed; she slipped away as if she were glad of the opportunity.'

I thought of the Countess of Carberry and felt that history repeated itself.

'She was one of the old stock,' continued Captain Littlepage, with touching sincerity. 'She was very much looked up to in this town, and will be missed.'

I wondered, as I looked at him, if he had sprung from a line of ministers; he had the refinement of look and air of command which are the heritage of the old ecclesiastical families of New England. But as Darwin says in his autobiography, 'there is no such king as a sea-captain; he is greater even than a king or a school-master!'

Captain Littlepage moved his chair out of the wake of the sunshine, and still sat looking at me. I began to be very eager to know upon what errand he had come.

'It may be found out some o' these days,' he said earnestly. 'We may know it all, the next step; where Mrs. Begg is now, for instance. Certainty, not conjecture, is what we all desire.'

'I suppose we shall know it all some day,' said I.

'We shall know it while yet below,' insisted the captain, with a flush of impatience on his thin cheeks. 'We have not looked for truth in the right direction. I know what I speak of; those who have laughed at me

34

little know how much reason my ideas are based upon.' He waved his hand toward the village below. 'In that handful of houses they fancy that they comprehend the universe.'

I smiled, and waited for him to go on.

'I am an old man, as you can see,' he continued, 'and I have been a shipmaster the greater part of my life – forty-three years in all. You may not think it, but I am above eighty years of age.'

He did not look so old, and I hastened to say so.

'You must have left the sea a good many years ago, then, Captain Littlepage?' I said.

'I should have been serviceable at least five or six years more,' he answered. 'My acquaintance with certain – my experience upon a certain occasion, I might say, gave rise to prejudice. I do not mind telling you that I chanced to learn of one of the greatest discoveries that man has ever made.'

Now we were approaching dangerous ground, but a sudden sense of his sufferings at the hands of the ignorant came to my help, and I asked to hear more with all the deference I really felt. A swallow flew into the schoolhouse at this moment as if a kingbird were after it, and beat itself against the walls for a minute, and escaped again to the open air; but Captain Littlepage took no notice whatever of the flurry.

'I had a valuable cargo of general merchandise from the London Docks to Fort Churchill, a station of the old company on Hudson's Bay,' said the captain ear-

35

nestly. 'We were delayed in lading, and baffled by
head winds and a heavy tumbling sea all the way
north about and across. Then the fog kept us off the
coast; and when I made port at last, it was too late to
delay in those northern waters with such a vessel and
such a crew as I had. They cared for nothing, and
idled me into a fit of sickness; but my first mate was a
good, excellent man, with no more idea of being frozen
in there until spring than I had, so we made what speed
we could to get clear of Hudson's Bay and off the coast.
I owned an eighth of the vessel, and he owned a six-
teenth of her. She was a full-rigged ship, called the
Minerva, but she was getting old and leaky. I meant
it should be my last v'y'ge in her, and so it proved. She
had been an excellent vessel in her day. Of the cowards
aboard her I can't say so much.'

'Then you were wrecked?' I asked, as he made a long
pause.

'I wa'n't caught astern o' the lighter by any fault of
mine,' said the captain gloomily. 'We left Fort Church-
hill and run out into the Bay with a light pair o' heels;
but I had been vexed to death with their red-tape
rigging at the company's office, and chilled with stayin'
on deck an' tryin' to hurry up things, and when we were
well out o' sight o' land, headin' for Hudson's Straits,
I had a bad turn o' some sort o' fever, and had to stay
below. The days were getting short, and we made
good runs, all well on board but me, and the crew done
their work by dint of hard driving.'

I began to find this unexpected narrative a little dull. Captain Littlepage spoke with a kind of slow correctness that lacked the longshore high flavour to which I had grown used; but I listened respectfully while he explained the winds having become contrary, and talked on in a dreary sort of way about his voyage, the bad weather, and the disadvantages he was under in the lightness of his ship, which bounced about like a chip in a bucket, and would not answer the rudder or properly respond to the most careful setting of sails.

'So there we were blowin' along anyways,' he complained; but looking at me at this moment, and seeing that my thoughts were unkindly wandering, he ceased to speak.

'It was a hard life at sea in those days, I am sure,' said I, with redoubled interest.

'It was a dog's life,' said the poor old gentleman, quite reassured, 'but it made men of those who followed it. I see a change for the worse even in our own town here; full of loafers now, small and poor as 't is, who once would have followed the sea, every lazy soul of 'em. There is no occupation so fit for just that class o' men who never get beyond the fo'cas'le. I view it, in addition, that a community narrows down and grows dreadful ignorant when it is shut up to its own affairs, and gets no knowledge of the outside world except from a cheap, unprincipled newspaper. In the old days, a good part o' the best men here knew a hundred ports and something of the way folks lived in them. They saw the world for themselves, and like's not their wives and children saw it with them. They may not have had the best of knowledge to carry with 'em sight-seein', but they were some acquainted with foreign lands an' their laws, an' could see outside the battle for town clerk here in Dunnet; they got some sense o' proportion. Yes, they lived more dignified, and their houses were better within an' without. Shipping's a terrible loss to this part o' New England from a social point o' view, ma'am.'

'I have thought of that myself,' I returned, with my interest quite awakened. 'It accounts for the change in a great many things, – the sad disappearance of sea-captains, – doesn't it?'

'A shipmaster was apt to get the habit of reading,' said my companion, brightening still more, and taking on a most touching air of unreserve. 'A captain is not expected to be familiar with his crew, and for company's sake in dull days and nights he turns to his book. Most of us old shipmasters came to know 'most every-thing about something; one would take to readin' on farming topics, and some were great on medicine, – but Lord help their poor crews! – or some were all for history, and now and then there'd be one like me that gave his time to the poets. I was well acquainted with a shipmaster that was all for bees an' bee-keepin'; and if you met him in port and went aboard, he'd sit and talk a terrible while about their havin' so much information, and the money that could be made out of keepin' em. He was one of the smartest captains that ever sailed the

38

seas, but they used to call the *Newcastle*, a great barque he commanded for many years, Tuttle's beehive. There was old Cap'n Jameson: he had notions of Solomon's Temple, and made a very handsome little model of the same, right from the Scripture measurements, same's other sailors make little ships and design new tricks of rigging and all that. No, there's nothing to take the place of shipping in a place like ours. These bicycles offend me dreadfully; they don't afford no real oppor-unities of experience such as a man gained on a voyage. No: when folks left home in the old days they left it to some purpose, and when they got home they stayed there and had some pride in it. There's no large-minded way of thinking now: the worst have got to be best and rule everything; we're all turned upside down and going back year by year.'

'Oh, no, Captain Littlepage, I hope not,' said I, trying to soothe his feelings.

There was a silence in the schoolhouse, but we could hear the noise of the water on a beach below. It sounded like the strange warning wave that gives notice of the turn of the tide. A late golden robin, with the most joyful and eager of voices, was singing close by in a thicket of wild roses.

CHAPTER SIX

The Waiting Place

★

'How did you manage with the rest of that rough voyage on the *Minerva?*' I asked.

'I shall be glad to explain to you,' said Captain Littlepage, forgetting his grievances for the moment. 'If I had a map at hand I could explain better. We were driven to and fro 'way up toward what we used to call Parry's Discoveries, and lost our bearings. It was thick and foggy, and at last I lost my ship; she drove on a rock, and we managed to get ashore on what I took to be a barren island, the few of us that were left alive. When she first struck, the sea was somewhat calmer than it had been, and most of the crew, against orders, manned the long-boat and put off in a hurry, and were never heard of more. Our own boat upset, but the carpenter kept himself and me above water, and we drifted in. I had no strength to call upon after my recent fever, and laid down to die; but he found the tracks of a man and dog the second day, and got along the shore to one of those far missionary stations that the Moravians support. They were very poor themselves, and in distress; 't was a useless place. There were but few Esquimaux left in that region. There we remained for some time, and I became acquainted with strange events.'

The captain lifted his head and gave me a questioning glance. I could not help noticing that the dulled look in his eyes had gone, and there was instead a clear intentness that made them seem dark and piercing.

'There was a supply ship expected, and the pastor, an excellent Christian man, made no doubt that we should get passage in her. He was hoping that orders would come to break up the station; but everything was uncertain, and we got on the best we could for a while. We fished, and helped the people in other ways; there was no other way of paying our debts. I was taken to the pastor's house until I got better; but they were crowded, and I felt myself in the way, and made excuse to join with an old seaman, a Scotchman, who had built him a warm cabin, and had room in it for another. He was looked upon with regard, and had stood by the pastor in some troubles with the people. He had been on one of those English exploring parties that found one end of the road to the north pole, but never could find the other. We lived like dogs in a kennel, or so you'd have thought if you had seen the hut from the outside; but the main thing was to keep warm; there were piles of bird-skins to lie on, and he'd made him a good bunk, and there was another for me. 'T was dreadful dreary waitin' there; we begun to think the supply steamer was lost, and my poor ship broke up and strewed herself all along the shore. We got to watching on the headlands; my men and me knew the people were short of supplies and had to pinch themselves. It ought to read in the Bible, "Man cannot live by fish alone," if they'd told the truth of things; 'taint bread that wears the worst on you! First part of the time, old Gaffett, that I lived with, seemed speechless, and I didn't know what to make of him, nor he of me, I daresay; but as we got acquainted, I found he'd been through more disasters than I had, and had troubles that wa'n't going to let him live a great while. It used to ease his mind to talk to an understanding person, so we used to sit and talk together all day, if it rained or blew so that we couldn't get out. I'd got a bad blow on the back of my head at the time we came ashore, and it pained me at times, and my strength was broken, anyway; I've never been so able since.'

Captain Littlepage fell into a reverie.

'Then I had the good of my reading,' he explained presently. 'I had no books; the pastor spoke but little English, and all his books were foreign; but I used to say over all I could remember. The old poets little knew what comfort they could be to a man. I was well acquainted with the works of Milton, but up there it did seem to me as if Shakespeare was the king; he has his sea terms very accurate, and some beautiful passages were calming to the mind. I could say them over until I shed tears; there was nothing beautiful to me in that place but the stars above and those passages of verse.

'Gaffett was always brooding and brooding and talking to himself; he was afraid he should never get away, and it preyed upon his mind. He thought when I got home

I could interest the scientific men in his discovery:
but they're all taken up with their own notions; some
didn't even take pains to answer the letters I wrote.
You observe that I said this crippled man Gaffett had
been shipped on a voyage of discovery. I now tell you
that the ship was lost on its return, and only Gaffett
and two officers were saved off the Greenland coast, and
he had knowledge later that those men never got back
to England; the brig they shipped on was run down in
the night. So no other living soul had the facts, and he
gave them to me. There is a strange sort of a country
'way up north beyond the ice, and strange folks living
in it. Gaffett believed it was the next world to this.'

'What do you mean, Captain Littlepage?' I exclaimed.
The old man was bending forward and whispering; he
looked over his shoulder before he spoke the last
sentence.

'To hear old Gaffett tell about it was something
awful,' he said, going on with his story quite steadily
after the moment of excitement had passed. ''T was
first a tale of dogs and sledges, and cold and wind and
snow. Then they begun to find the ice grow rotten;
they had been frozen in, and got into a current flowing
north, far up beyond Fox Channel, and they took to
their boats when the ship got crushed, and this warm
current took them out of sight of the ice, and into a great
open sea; and they still followed it due north, just the
very way they had planned to go. Then they struck a
coast that wasn't laid down or charted, but the cliffs

43

were such that no boat could land until they found a bay and struck across under sail to the other side where the shore looked lower; they were scant of provisions and out of water, but they got sight of something that looked like a great town. "For God's sake, Gaffett!" said I, the first time he told me. "You don't mean a town two degrees farther north than ships had ever been?" for he'd got their course marked on an old chart that he'd pieced out at the top; but he insisted upon it, and told it over and over again, to be sure I had it straight to carry to those who would be interested. There was no snow and ice, he said, after they had sailed some days with that warm current, which seemed to come right from under the ice that they'd been pinched up in and had been crossing on foot for weeks.'

'But what about the town?' I asked. 'Did they get to the town?'

'They did,' said the captain, 'and found inhabitants; 't was an awful condition of things. It appeared, as near as Gaffett could express it, like a place where there was neither living nor dead. They could see the place when they were approaching it by sea pretty near like any town, and thick with habitations; but all at once they lost sight of it altogether, and when they got close inshore they could see the shapes of folks, but they never could get near them, — all blowing gray figures that would pass along alone, or sometimes gathered in companies as if they were watching. The men were frightened at first, but the shapes never came near

44

them, – it was as if they blew back; and at last they all got bold and went ashore, and found birds' eggs and sea fowl, like any wild northern spot where creatures were tame and folks had never been, and there was good water. Gaffett said that he and another man came near one o' the fog-shaped men that was going along slow with the look of a pack on his back, among the rocks, an' they chased him; but, Lord! he flittered away out o' sight like a leaf the wind takes with it, or a piece of cobweb. They would make as if they talked together, but there was no sound of voices, and "they acted as if they didn't see us, but only felt us coming towards them," says Gaffett one day, trying to tell the particulars. They couldn't see the town when they were ashore. One day the captain and the doctor were gone till night up across the high land where the town had seemed to be, and they came back at night beat out and white as ashes, and wrote and wrote all next day in their note-books, and whispered together full of excitement, and they were sharp-spoken with the men when they offered to ask any questions.

'Then there came a day,' said Captain Littlepage, leaning toward me with a strange look in his eyes, and whispering quickly. 'The men all swore they wouldn't stay any longer; the man on watch early in the morning gave the alarm, and they all put off in the boat and got a little way out to sea. Those folks, or whatever they were, come about 'em like bats; all at once they raised incessant armies, and come as if to drive 'em back to sea. They stood thick at the edge o' the water like the ridges o' grim war; no thought o' flight, none of retreat. Sometimes a standing fight, then soaring on main wing tormented all the air. And when they'd got the boat out o' reach o' danger, Gaffett said they looked back, and there was the town again, standing up just as they'd seen it first, comin' on the coast. Say what you might, they all believed 't was a kind of waiting-place between this world an' the next.'

The captain had sprung to his feet in his excitement, and made excited gestures, but he still whispered huskily.

'Sit down, sir,' I said as quietly as I could, and he sank into his seat, quite spent.

'Gaffett thought the officers were hurrying home to report and to fit out a new expedition when they were all lost. At the time, the men got orders not to talk over what they had seen,' the old man explained presently in a more natural tone.

'Weren't they all starving, and wasn't it a mirage or something of that sort?' I ventured to ask. But he looked at me blankly.

'Gaffett had got so that his mind ran on nothing else,' he went on. 'The ship's surgeon let fall an opinion to the captain, one day, that 't was some condition o' the light and the magnetic currents that let them see those folks. 'Twan't a right-feeling part of the world, any-way; they had to battle with the compass to make it serve, an' everything seemed to go wrong. Gaffett had

46

worked it out in his own mind that they was all common ghosts, but the conditions were unusual favourable for seeing them. He was always talking about the Ge'graphical Society, but he never took proper steps, as I view it now, and stayed right there at the mission. He was a good deal crippled, and thought they'd confine him in some jail of a hospital. He said he was waiting to find the right men to tell, somebody bound north. Once in a while they stopped there to leave a mail or something. He was set in his notions, and let two or three proper explorin' expeditions go by him because he didn't like their looks; but when I was there he had got restless, fearin' he might be taken away or something. He had all his directions written out straight as a string to give the right ones. I wanted him to trust 'em to me, so I might have something to show, but he wouldn't. I suppose he's dead now. I wrote to him, an' I done all I could. 'Twill be a great exploit some o' these days.'

I assented absent-mindedly, thinking more just then of my companion's alert, determined look and the seafaring, ready aspect that had come to his face; but at this moment there fell a sudden change, and the old, pathetic, scholarly look returned. Behind me hung a a map of North America, and I saw, as I turned a little, that his eyes were fixed upon the northernmost regions and their careful recent outlines with a look of bewilderment.

CHAPTER SEVEN

The Outer Island

★

GAFFETT with his good bunk and the bird-skins, the story of the wreck of the *Minerva*, the human-shaped creatures of fog and cobweb, the great words of Milton with which he described their onslaught upon the crew, all this moving tale had such an air of truth that I could not argue with Captain Littlepage. The old man looked away from the map as if it had vaguely troubled him, and regarded me appealingly.

'We were just speaking of' – and he stopped. I saw that he had suddenly forgotten his subject.

'There were a great many persons at the funeral,' I hastened to say.

'Oh, yes,' the captain answered, with satisfaction. 'All showed respect who could. The sad circumstances had for a moment slipped my mind. Yes, Mrs. Begg will be very much missed. She was a capital manager for her husband when he was at sea. Oh, yes, shipping is a very great loss.' And he sighed heavily. 'There was hardly a man of any standing who didn't interest himself in some way in navigation. It always gave credit to a town. I call it low-water mark now here in Dunnet.'

He rose with dignity to take leave, and asked me to stop at his house some day, when he would show me some outlandish things that he had brought home from sea. I was familiar with the subject of the decadence of shipping interests in all its affecting branches, having been already some time in Dunnet, and I felt sure that Captain Littlepage's mind had now returned to a safe level.

As we came down the hill toward the village our ways divided, and when I had seen the old captain well started on a smooth piece of sidewalk which would lead him to his own door, we parted, the best of friends. 'Step in some afternoon,' he said, as affectionately as if I were a fellow-shipmaster wrecked on the lee shore of age like himself. I turned toward home, and presently met Mrs. Todd coming toward me with an anxious expression.

'I see you sleevin' the old gentleman down the hill,' she suggested.

'Yes. I've had a very interesting afternoon with him,' I answered; and her face brightened.

'Oh, then he's all right. I was afraid 'twas one o' his flighty spells, an' Mari' Harris wouldn't – '

'Yes,' I returned, smiling, 'he has been telling me some old stories, but we talked about Mrs. Begg and the funeral beside, and Paradise Lost.'

'I expect he got tellin' of you some o' his great narratives,' she answered, looking at me shrewdly. 'Funerals always sets him goin'. Some o' them tales hangs together toler'ble well,' she added, with a sharper look than before. 'An' he's been a great reader all his seafarin' days. Some thinks he overdid, and affected his head, but for a man o' his years he's amazin' now when he's at his best. Oh, he used to be a beautiful man!'

We were standing where there was fine view of the harbour and its long stretches of shore all covered by the great army of pointed firs, darkly cloaked and standing as if they waited to embark. As we looked far seaward among the outer islands, the trees seemed to march seaward still, going steadily over the heights and down to the water's edge.

It had been growing gray and cloudy, like the first evening of autumn, and a shadow had fallen on the darkening shore. Suddenly, as we looked, a gleam of golden sunshine struck the outer islands, and one of them shone out clear in the light, and revealed itself in a compelling way to our eyes. Mrs. Todd was looking off across the bay with a face full of affection and interest. The sunburst upon that outermost island made it seem like a sudden revelation of the world beyond this which some believe to be so near.

'That's where mother lives,' said Mrs. Todd. 'Can't we see it plain? I was brought up out there on Green Island. I know every rock an' bush on it.'

'Your mother!' I exclaimed, with great interest.

'Yes, dear, cert'in; I've got her yet, old's I be. She's one of them spry, light-footed little women; always was, an' light-hearted, too,' answered Mrs. Todd, with satisfaction. 'She's seen all the trouble folks can see, without it's her last sickness; an' she's got a word of courage for everybody. Life ain't spoilt her a mite. She's eighty-six an' I'm sixty-seven, and I've seen the time I've felt a good sight the oldest. "Land sakes alive!" says she, last time I was out to see her. "How you do lurch about steppin' into a bo't!' I laughed so I liked to have gone right over into the water; an' we pushed off, an' left her laughin' there on the shore.'

The light had faded as we watched. Mrs. Todd had mounted a gray rock, and stood there grand and architectural, like a *caryatide*. Presently she stepped down, and we continued our way homeward.

'You an' me, we'll take a bo't an' go out some day and see mother,' she promised me. "T would please her very much, an' there's one or two sca'ce herbs grows better on the island than anywheres else. I ain't seen their like nowheres here on the main.

'Now I'm goin' right down to get us each a mug o' my beer,' she announced as we entered the house, 'an' I believe I'll sneak in a little mite o' camomile. Goin' to the funeral an' all, I feel to have had a very wearin' afternoon.'

I heard her going down into the cool little cellar, and then there was considerable delay. When she returned, mug in hand, I noticed the taste of camomile, in spite of my protest; but its flavour was disguised by some other herb that I did not know, and she stood over me until I drank it all and said that I liked it.

'I don't give that to everybody,' said Mrs. Todd kindly; and I felt for a moment as if it were part of a spell and incantation, and as if my enchantress would now begin to look like the cobweb shapes of the arctic town. Nothing happened but a quiet evening and some delightful plans that we made about going to Green Island, and on the morrow there was the clear sunshine and blue sky of another day.

CHAPTER EIGHT

Green Island

★

ONE morning, very early, I heard Mrs. Todd in the garden outside my window. By the unusual loudness of her remarks to a passer-by and the notes of a familiar hymn which she sang as she worked among the herbs, and which came as if directed purposely to the sleepy ears of my consciousness, I knew that she wished I would wake up and come and speak to her.

In a few minutes she responded to a morning voice from behind the blinds. 'I expect you're goin' up to your schoolhouse to pass all this pleasant day; yes, I expect you're goin' to be dreadful busy,' she said despairingly.

'Perhaps not,' said I. 'Why, what's going to be the matter with you, Mrs. Todd?' For I supposed that she was tempted by the fine weather to take one of her favourite expeditions along the shore pastures to gather herbs and simples, and would like to have me keep the house.

'No, I don't want to go nowhere by land,' she answered gaily, – 'no, not by land; but I don't know's we shall have a better day all the rest of the summer to go out to Green Island an' see mother. I waked up early thinkin' of her. The wind's light north-east, – it will take us right straight out; an' this time o' year 't's liable to change round south-west an' fetch us home pretty, 'long late in the afternoon. Yes, it's goin' to be a good day.'

'Speak to the captain and the Bowden boy, if you see anybody going by toward the landing,' said I. 'We'll take the big boat.'

'Oh, my sakes! now you let me do things my way,' said Mrs. Todd scornfully. 'No, dear, we won't take no big bo't. I'll just git a handy dory, an' Johnny Bowden an' me, we'll man her ourselves. I don't want no abler b'ot than a good dory, an' a nice light breeze ain't goin' to make no sea; an' Johnny's my cousin's son, – mother'll like to have him come; an' he'll be down to the herrin' weirs all the time we're there, anyway; we don't want to carry no men folks havin' to be considered every minute an' takin' up all our time. No, you let me do; we'll just slip out an' see mother by ourselves. I guess what breakfast you'll want's about ready now.'

I had become well acquainted with Mrs. Todd as landlady, herb-gatherer, and rustic philosopher; we had been discreet fellow-passengers once or twice when I had sailed up the coast to a larger town than Dunnet Landing to do some shopping; but I was yet to become acquainted with her as a mariner. An hour later we pushed off from the landing in the desired dory. The tide was just on the turn, beginning to fall, and several friends and acquaintances stood along the side of the dilapidated wharf and cheered us by their words and evident interest. Johnny Bowden and I were both rowing in haste to get out where we could catch the breeze and put up the small sail which lay clumsily furled along the gunwale. Mrs. Todd sat aft, a stern and unbending lawgiver.

'You better let her drift; we'll get there 'bout as quick; the tide'll take her right out from under these old buildin's; there's plenty wind outside.'

'Your bo't ain't trimmed proper, Mis' Todd!' exclaimed a voice from shore. 'You're lo'ded so the bo't 'll drag; you can't git her before the wind, ma'am. You set 'midships, Mis' Todd, an' let the boy hold the sheet 'n' steer after he gits the sail up; you won't never git out to Green Island that way. She's lo'ded bad, your bo't is, – she's heavy behind's she is now!'

Mrs. Todd turned with some difficulty and regarded the anxious adviser, my right oar flew out of water, and we seemed about to capsize. 'That you, Asa? Good-mornin',' she said politely. 'I al'ays liked the starn seat best. When 'd you git back from up country?'

This allusion to Asa's origin was not lost upon the rest of the company. We were some little distance from shore, but we could hear a chuckle of laughter, and Asa, a person who was too ready with his criticism and advice on every possible subject, turned and walked indignantly away.

When we caught the wind we were soon on our seaward course, and only stopped to underrun a trawl, for the floats of which Mrs. Todd looked earnestly, explaining that her mother might not be prepared for three extra to dinner; it was her brother's trawl, and she meant to just run her eye along for the right sort of a little haddock. I leaned over the boat's side with great interest and excitement, while she skilfully handled the long line of hooks, and made scornful remarks upon worthless, bait-consuming creatures of the sea as she reviewed them and left them on the trawl or shook them off into the waves. At last we came to what she pronounced a proper haddock, and having taken him on board and ended his life resolutely, we went our way.

As we sailed along I listened to an increasingly delightful commentary upon the islands, some of them barren rocks, or at best giving sparse pasturage for sheep in the early summer. On one of these an eager little flock ran to the water's edge and bleated at us so affectingly that I would willingly have stopped; but Mrs. Todd steered away from the rocks, and scolded at the sheep's mean owner, an acquaintance of hers, who grudged the little salt and still less care which the patient creatures needed. The hot midsummer sun makes prisons of these small islands that are a paradise in early June, with their cool springs and short thick-growing grass. On a larger island, farther out to sea, my entertaining companion showed me with glee the small houses of two farmers who shared the island between them, and declared that for three generations the people had not spoken to each other even in times of sickness or death or birth. 'When the news come that the war was over, one of 'em knew it a week, and never stepped across to his wall to tell the others,' she said. 'There, they enjoy it: they've got to have somethin' to interest 'em in such a place; 'tis a good deal more trying' to be tied to folks you don't like than 'tis to be alone. Each of 'em tells the neighbours their wrongs; plenty likes to hear and tell again; them as fetch a bone'll carry one, an' so they keep the fight a-goin'. I must say I like variety myself; some folks washes Monday an' irons Tuesday the whole year round, even if the circus is goin' by!'

A long time before we landed at Green Island we could see the small white house, standing high like a beacon, where Mrs. Todd was born and where her mother lived, on a green slope above the water, with dark spruce woods still higher. There were crops in the fields, which we presently distinguished from one another. Mrs. Todd examined them while we were still far at sea. 'Mother's late potatoes looks backwards; ain't had rain enough so far,' she pronounced her opinion. 'They look weedier than what they call Front Street down to Cowper Centre. I expect brother William is so occupied with his herrin' weirs an' servin' out bait to the schooners that he don't think once a day of the land.'

'What's the flag for, up above the spruces there behind the house?' I inquired, with eagerness.

'Oh, that's the sign for herrin',' she explained kindly, while Johnny Bowden regarded me with contemptuous surprise. 'When they get enough for schooners they raise that flag; an' when 't is a poor catch in the weir pocket they just fly a little signal down by the shore, an' then the small bo'ts comes and get enough an' over for their trawls. There, look! there she is: mother sees us; she's wavin' somethin' out o' the fore door! She'll be to the landin'-place quick's we are.'

I looked, and could see a tiny flutter in the doorway, but a quicker signal had made its way from the heart on shore to the heart on the sea.

'How do you suppose she knows it's me?' said Mrs. Todd, with a tender smile on her broad face. 'There, you never get over bein' a child long's you have a mother to go to. Look at the chimney now; she's gone right in an' brightened up the fire. Well, there, I'm glad mother's well; you'll enjoy seein' her very much.'

Mrs. Todd leaned back into her proper position, and the boat trimmed again. She took a firmer grasp of the sheet, and gave an impatient look up at the gaff and the leech of the little sail, and twitched the sheet as if she urged the wind like a horse. There came at once a fresh gust, and we seemed to have doubled our speed. Soon we were near enough to see a tiny figure with handkerchiefed head come down across the field and stand waiting for us at the cove above a curve of pebble beach.

Presently the dory grated on the pebbles, and Johnny Bowden, who had been kept in abeyance during the voyage, sprang out and used manful exertions to haul us up with the next wave, so that Mrs. Todd could make a dry landing.

'You done that very well,' she said, mounting to her feet, and coming ashore somewhat stiffly, but with great dignity, refusing our outstretched hands, and returning to possess herself of a bag which had lain at her feet.

'Well, mother, here I be!' she announced with indifference; but they stood and beamed in each other's faces.

'Lookin' pretty well for an old lady, ain't she?' said Mrs. Todd's mother, turning away from her daughter to speak to me. She was a delightful little person herself, with bright eyes and an affectionate air of expectation like a child on a holiday. You felt as if Mrs. Blackett were an old and dear friend before you let go her cordial hand. We all started together up the hill.

'Now don't you haste too fast, mother,' said Mrs. Todd warningly; ''tis a far reach o' risin' ground to the fore door, and you won't set an' get your breath when you're once there, but go trotting about. Now don't you go a mite faster than we proceed with this bag an' basket. Johnny, there, 'll fetch up the haddock. I just made one stop to underrun William's trawl till I come to jes' such a fish's I thought you'd want to make one o' your nice chowders of. I've brought an onion with me that was layin' about on the window-sill at home.'

'That's just what I was wantin',' said the hostess. 'I give a sigh when you spoke o' chowder, knowin' my onions was out. William forgot to replenish us last time he was to the Landin'. Don't you haste so yourself, Almiry, up this risin' ground. I hear you commencin' to wheeze a'ready.'

This mild revenge seemed to afford great pleasure to both giver and receiver. They laughed a little, and looked at each other affectionately, and then at me. Mrs. Todd considerately paused, and faced about to regard the wide sea view. I was glad to stop, being more out of breath than either of my companions, and I prolonged the halt by asking the names of the neighbouring islands. There was a fine breeze blowing, which we felt more there on the high land than when we were running before it in the dory.

'Why, this ain't that kitten I saw when I was out last, the one that I said didn't appear likely?' exclaimed Mrs. Todd as we went our way.

'That's the one, Almiry,' said her mother. 'She always had a likely look to me, an' she's right after her business. I never see such a mouser for one of her age. If 'twan't for William, I never should have housed that other dronin' old thing so long; but he sets by her on account of her havin' a bob tail. I don't deem it advisable to maintain cats just on account of their havin' bob tails; they're like all other curiosities, good for them that wants to see 'em twice. This kitten catches mice for both, an' keeps me respectable as I ain't been for a year. She's a real understandin' little help, this kitten is. I picked her from among five Miss Augusta Pennell had over to Burnt Island,' said the old woman, trudging along with the kitten close at her skirts. 'Augusta, she says to me, "Why, Mis' Blackett, you've took the homeliest"; an' says I, "I've got the smartest; I'm satisfied."'

'I'd trust nobody sooner'n you to pick out a kitten, mother,' said the daughter handsomely, and we went on in peace and harmony.

The house was just before us now, on a green level that looked as if a huge hand had scooped it out of the long green field we had been ascending. A little way above, the dark spruce woods began to climb the top of the hill and cover the seaward slopes of the island. There was just room for the small farm and the forest; we looked down at the fish-house and its rough sheds, and the weirs stretching far out into the water. As we looked upward, the tops of the firs came sharp against the blue sky. There was a great stretch of rough pasture land round the shoulder of the island to the eastward, and here were all the thick-scattered gray rocks that kept their places, and the gray backs of many sheep that forever wandered and fed on the thin sweet pasturage that fringed the ledges and made soft hollows and strips of green turf like growing velvet. I could see the rich green of bayberry bushes here and there, where the rocks made room. The air was very sweet; one could not help wishing to be a citizen of such a complete and tiny continent and home of fisherfolk.

The house was broad and clean, with a roof that

looked heavy on its low walls. It was one of the houses that seem firm-rooted in the ground, as if they were two-thirds below the surface, like icebergs. The front door stood hospitably open in expectation of company, and an orderly vine grew at each side ; but our path led to the kitchen door at the house-end, and there grew a mass of gay flowers and greenery, as if they had been swept together by some diligent garden broom into a tangled heap: there were portulacas all along under the lower step and straggling off into the grass, and clustering mallows that crept as near as they dared, like poor relations. I saw the bright eyes and brainless little heads of two half-grown chickens who were snuggled down among the mallows as if they had been chased away from the door more than once, and expected to be again.

'It seems kind o' formal comin' in this way,' said Mrs. Todd impulsively, as we passed the flowers and came to the front doorstep; but she was mindful of the proprieties, and walked before us into the best room on the left.

'Why, mother, if you haven't gone an' turned the carpet!' she exclaimed, with something in her voice that spoke of awe and admiration. 'When'd you get to it? I s'pose Mis' Addicks come over an' helped you, from White Island Landing?'

'No, she didn't,' answered the old woman, standing proudly erect, and making the most of a great moment. 'I done it all myself with William's help. He had a spare day, an' took right holt with me; an' 't was all well beat on the grass, an' turned, an' put down again afore we went to bed. I ripped an' sewed over two o' them long breadths. I ain't had such a good night's sleep for two years.'

'There, what do you think o' havin' such a mother as that for eighty-six year old?' said Mrs. Todd, standing before us like a large figure of Victory.

As for the mother, she took on a sudden look of youth; you felt as if she promised a great future, and was beginning, not ending, her summers and their happy toils.

'My, my!' exclaimed Mrs. Todd. 'I couldn't ha' done it myself, I've got to own it.'

'I was much pleased to have it off my mind,' said Mrs. Blackett, humbly; 'the more so because along at the first of the next week I wasn't very well. I suppose it may have been the change of weather.'

Mrs. Todd could not resist a significant glance at me, but, with charming sympathy, she forbore to point the lesson or to connect this illness with its apparent cause. She loomed larger than ever in the little old-fashioned best room, with its few pieces of good furniture and pictures of national interest. The green paper curtains were stamped with conventional landscapes of a foreign order, — castles on inaccessible crags, and lovely lakes with steep wooded shores; under-foot the treasured carpet was covered thick with home-made rugs. There were empty glass lamps and crystallised bouquets of grass and some fine shells on the narrow mantelpiece.

'I was married in this room,' said Mrs. Todd unexpectedly; and I heard her give a sigh after she had spoken, as if she could not help the touch of regret that would forever come with all her thoughts of happiness.

'We stood right there between the windows,' she added, 'and the minister stood here. William wouldn't come in. He was always odd about seein' folks, just's he is now. I run to meet 'em from a child, an' William, he'd take an' run away.'

'I've been the gainer,' said the old mother cheerfully. 'William has been son an' daughter both since you was married off the island. He's been 'most too satisfied to stop at home 'long o' his old mother, but I always tell 'em I'm the gainer.'

We were all moving toward the kitchen as if by common instinct. The best room was too suggestive of serious occasions, and the shades were all pulled down to shut out the summer light and air. It was indeed a tribute to Society to find a room set apart for her behests out there on so apparently neighbourless and remote an island. Afternoon visits and evening festivals must be few in such a bleak situation at certain seasons of the year, but Mrs. Blackett was of those who do not live to themselves, and who have long since passed the line that divides mere self-concern from a valued share in whatever Society can give and take. There were those of her neighbours who never had taken the trouble to furnish a best room, but Mrs. Blackett was one who knew the uses of a parlour.

'Yes, do come right out into the old kitchen; I shan't make any stranger of you,' she invited us pleasantly, after we had been properly received in the room appointed to formality. 'I expect A!miry, here, 'll be driftin' out 'mongst the pasture- weeds quick's she can find a good excuse. 'T is hot now. You'd better content yourselves till you get nice an' rested, an' 'long after dinner the sea-breeze'll spring up, an' then you can take your walks, an' go up an' see the prospect from the big ledge. Almiry 'll want to show off everything there is. Then I'll get you a good cup o' tea before you start to go home. The days are plenty long now.'

While we were talking in the best room the selected fish had been mysteriously brought up from the shore, and lay all cleaned and ready in an earthen crock on the table.

'I think William might have just stopped an said a word,' remarked Mrs. Todd, pouting with high affront as she caught sight of it. 'He's friendly enough when he comes ashore, an' was remarkable social the last time, for him.'

'He ain't disposed to be very social with the ladies,' explained William's mother, with a delightful glance at me, as if she counted upon my friendship and tolerance. 'He's very particular, and he's all in his old fishin'-clothes to-day. He'll want me to tell him everything you said and done, after you've gone. William has very deep affections. He'll want to see you, Almiry. Yes, I guess he'll be in by an' by.'

'I'll search for him by 'n' by, if he don't,' proclaimed Mrs. Todd, with an air of unalterable resolution. 'I know all of his burrows down 'long the shore. I'll catch him by hand 'fore he knows it. I've got some business with William, anyway. I brought forty-two cents with me that was due him for them last lobsters he brought in.'

'You can leave it with me,' suggested the little old mother, who was already stepping about among her pots and pans in the pantry, and preparing to make the chowder.

I became possessed of a sudden unwonted curiosity in regard to William, and felt that half the pleasure of my visit would be lost if I could not make his interesting acquaintance.

CHAPTER NINE

William

*

Mrs. Todd had taken the onion out of her basket and laid it down upon the kitchen table. 'There's Johnny Bowden come with us, you know,' she reminded her mother. 'He'll be hungry enough to eat his size.'

'I've got new doughnuts, dear,' said the little old lady. 'You don't often catch William 'n' me out o' provisions. I expect you might have chose a somewhat larger fish, but I'll try an' make it do. I shall have to have a few extra potatoes, but there's a field full out there, an' the hoe's leanin' against the well-house, in 'mongst the climbin'-beans.' She smiled, and gave her daughter a commanding nod.

'Land sakes alive! Let's blow the horn for William,' insisted Mrs. Todd, with some excitement. 'He needn't break his spirit so far's to come in. He'll know you need him for something particular, an' then we can call to him as he comes up the path. I won't put him to no pain.'

Mrs. Blackett's old face, for the first time, wore a look of trouble, and I found it necessary to counteract the teasing spirit of Almira. It was too pleasant to stay indoors altogether, even in such rewarding companionship; besides, I might meet William; and, straying out presently, I found the hoe by the well-house and an old splint basket at the woodshed door, and also found my way down to the field where there was a great square patch of rough, weedy potato-tops and tall ragweed. One corner was already dug, and I chose a fat-looking hill where the tops were well withered. There is all the pleasure that one can have in gold-digging in finding one's hopes satisfied in the riches of a good hill of potatoes. I longed to go on ; but it did not seem frugal to dig any longer after my basket was full, and at last I took my hoe by the middle and lifted the basket to go back up the hill. I was sure that Mrs. Blackett must be waiting impatiently to slice the potatoes into the chowder, layer after layer, with the fish.

'You let me take holt o' that basket, ma'am,' said a pleasant, anxious voice behind me.

I turned, startled in the silence of the wide field, and saw an elderly man, bent in the shoulders as fisher-men often are, grey-headed and clean-shaven, and with a timid air. It was William. He looked just like his mother, and I had been imagining that he was large and stout like his sister, Almira Todd; and, strange to say, my fancy had led me to picture him not far from thirty and a little loutish. It was necessary instead to pay William the respect due to age.

I accustomed myself to plain facts on the instant, and we said good-morning like old friends. The basket was really heavy, and I put the hoe through its handle and offered him one end; then we moved easily toward the house together, speaking of the fine weather and of mackerel which were reported to be striking in all about the bay. William had been out since three o'clock, and had taken an extra fare of fish. I could feel that Mrs. Todd's eyes were upon us as we approached the house, and although I fell behind in the narrow path, and let William take the basket alone and precede me at some little distance the rest of the way, I could plainly hear her greet him.

'Got round to comin' in, didn't you?' she inquired, with amusement. 'Well, now, that's clever. Didn't know 's I should see you to-day, William, an' I wanted to settle an account.'

I felt somewhat disturbed and responsible, but when I joined them they were on most simple and friendly terms. It became evident that, with William, it was the first step that cost, and that, having once joined in social interests, he was able to pursue them with more or less pleasure. He was about sixty, and not young-looking for his years, yet so undying is the spirit of youth, and bashfulness has such a power of survival, that I felt all the time as if one must try to make the occasion easy for some one who was young and new to the affairs of social life. He asked politely if I would like to go up to the great ledge while dinner was getting ready; so, not without a deep sense of pleasure, and a delighted look of surprise from the two hostesses, we started, William and I, as if both of us felt much younger than we looked. Such was the innocence and simplicity of the moment that when I heard Mrs. Todd laughing behind us in the kitchen I laughed too, but

William did not even blush. I think he was a little deaf, and he stepped along before me most business-like and intent upon his errand.

We went from the upper edge of the field above the house into a smooth, brown path among the dark spruces. The hot sun brought out the fragrance of the pitchy bark, and the shade was pleasant as we climbed the hill. William stopped once or twice to show me a great wasps'-nest close by, or some fishhawks'-nests below in a bit of swamp. He picked a few sprigs of late-blooming linnæa as we came out upon an open bit of pasture at the top of the island, and gave them to me without speaking, but he knew as well as I that one could not say half he wished about linnæa. Through this piece of rough pasture ran a huge shape of stone like the great backbone of an enormous creature. At the end, near the woods, we could climb up on it and walk along to the highest point; there above the circle of pointed firs we could look down over all the island, and could see the ocean that circled this and a hundred other bits of island-ground, the mainland shore and all the far horizons. It gave a sudden sense of space, for nothing stopped the eye or hedged one in,—that sense of liberty in space and time which great prospects always give.

'There ain't no such view in the world, I expect,' said William proudly, and I hastened to speak my heartfelt tribute of praise: it was impossible not to feel as if an untravelled boy had spoken, and yet one loved to have him value his native heath.

CHAPTER TEN

Where Pennyroyal Grew

★

We were a little late to dinner, but Mrs. Blackett and Mrs. Todd were lenient, and we all took our places after William had paused to wash his hands, like a pious Brahmin, at the well, and put on a neat blue coat which he took from a peg behind the kitchen door. Then he resolutely asked a blessing in words that I could not hear, and we ate the chowder and were thankful. The kitten went round and round the table, quite erect, and, holding on by her fierce young claws, she stopped to mew with pathos at each elbow, or darted off to the open door when a song sparrow forgot himself and lit in the grass too near. William did not talk much, but his sister Todd occupied the time and told all the news there was to tell of Dunnet Landing and its coasts, while the old mother listened with delight. Her hospitality was something exquisite; she had the gift which so many women lack, of being able to make themselves and their houses belong entirely to a guest's pleasure, – that charming surrender for the moment of themselves and whatever belongs to them, so that they make a part of one's own life that can never be forgotten. Tact is after all a kind of mind-reading, and my hostess held the golden gift. Sympathy is of the mind as well as the heart, and Mrs. Blackett's world and mine were one from the moment we met. Besides, she had that final, that highest gift of heaven, a perfect self-forgetfulness. Sometimes, as I watched her eager, sweet old face, I wondered why she had been set to shine on this lonely island of the northern coast. It must have been to keep the balance true, and make up to all her scattered and depending neighbours for other things which they may have lacked.

When we had finished clearing away the old blue plates, and the kitten had taken care of her share of the fresh haddock, just as we were putting back the kitchen chairs in their places, Mrs. Todd said briskly that she must go up into the pasture now to gather the desired herbs.

'You can stop here an' rest, or you can accompany me,' she announced. 'Mother ought to have her nap, and when we come back she an' William 'll sing for you. She admires music,' said Mrs. Todd, turning to speak to her mother.

But Mrs. Blackett tried to say that she couldn't sing as she used, and perhaps William wouldn't feel like it. She looked tired, the good old soul, or I should have liked to sit in the peaceful little house while she slept; I had had much pleasant experience of pastures already in her daughter's company. But it seemed best to go with Mrs. Todd, and off we went.

Mrs. Todd carried the gingham bag which she had brought from home, and a small heavy burden in the bottom made it hang straight and slender from her hand. The way was steep, and she soon grew breathless, so that we sat down to rest awhile on a convenient large stone among the bayberry.

'There, I wanted you to see this, — 't is mother's picture,' said Mrs. Todd; ''t was taken once when she was up to Portland, soon after she was married. That's me,' she added, opening another worn case, and displaying the full face of the cheerful child she looked like still in spite of being past sixty. 'And here's William an' father together. I take after father, large and heavy, an' William is like mother's folks, short an' thin. He ought to have made something o' himself bein' a man an' so like mother; but though he's been very steady to work, an' kept up the farm, an' done his fishin' too right along, he never had mother's snap an' power o' seein' things just as they be. He's got excellent judgment, too,' meditated William's sister, but she could not arrive at any satisfactory decision upon what she evidently thought his failure in life. 'I think it is well to see any one so happy an' makin' the most of life just as it falls to hand,' she said as she began to put the daguerreotypes away again; but I reached out my hand to see her mother's once more, a most flower-like face of a lovely young woman in quaint dress. There was in the eyes a look of anticipation and joy, a far-off look that sought the horizon; one often sees it in seafaring families, inherited by girls and boys alike from men who spend their lives at sea, and are always watching for distant sails or the first loom of the land. At sea there is nothing to be seen close by,

73   c*

and this has its counterpart in a sailor's character, in the large and brave and patient traits that are developed, the hopeful pleasantness that one loves so in a seafarer.

When the family pictures were wrapped again in a big handkerchief, we set forward in a narrow footpath and made our way to a lonely place that faced northward, where there was more pasturage and fewer bushes, and we went down to the edge of short grass above some rocky cliffs where the deep sea broke with a great noise, though the wind was down and the water looked quiet a little way from shore. Among the grass grew such pennyroyal as the rest of the world could not provide. There was a fine fragrance in the air as we gathered it sprig by sprig and stepped along carefully, and Mrs. Todd pressed her aromatic nosegay between her hands and offered it to me again and again.

'There's nothin' like it,' she said; 'oh no, there's no such pennyr'yal as this in the State of Maine. It's the right pattern of the plant, and all the rest I ever see is but an imitation. Don't it do you good?' And I answered with enthusiasm.

'There, dear, I never showed nobody else but mother where to find this place; 't is kind of sainted to me. Nathan, my husband, an' I used to love this place when we was courtin', and' – she hesitated, and then spoke softly – 'when he was lost, 't was just off shore tryin' to get in by the short channel out there between Squaw Islands, right in sight o' this headland where we'd set an' made our plans all summer long.'

I had never heard her speak of her husband before, but I felt that we were friends now since she had brought me to this place.

"T was but a dream with us,' Mrs. Todd said. 'I knew it when he was gone. I knew it'—and she whispered as if she were at confession—'I knew it afore he started to go to sea. My heart was gone out o' my keepin' before I ever saw Nathan; but he loved me well, and he made me real happy, and he died before he ever knew what he'd had to know if we'd lived long together. 'T is very strange about love. No, Nathan never found out, but my heart was troubled when I knew him first. There's more women likes to be loved than there is of those that loves. I spent some happy hours right here. I always liked Nathan, and he never knew. But this pennyr'yal always reminded me, as I'd sit and gather it and hear him talking'—it always would remind me of—the other one.'

She looked away from me, and presently rose and went on by herself. There was something lonely and solitary about her great determined shape. She might have been Antigone alone on the Theban plain. It is not often given in a noisy world to come to the places of great grief and silence. An absolute, archaic grief possessed this country-woman; she seemed like a renewal of some historic soul, with her sorrows and the remoteness of a daily life busied with rustic simplicities and the scents of primeval herbs.

I was not incompetent at herb-gathering, and after a while, when I had sat long enough waking myself to new thoughts, and reading a page of remembrance with new pleasure, I gathered some bunches, as I was bound to do, and at last we met again higher up the shore, in the plain every-day world we had left behind when we went down to the pennyroyal plot. As we walked together along the high edge of the field we saw a hundred sails about the bay and farther seaward; it was mid-afternoon or after, and the day was coming to an end.

'Yes, they're all makin' towards the shore, – the small craft an' the lobster smacks an' all,' said my companion. 'We must spend a little time with mother now, just to have our tea, an' then put for home.'

'No matter if we lose the wind at sundown; I can row in with Johnny,' said I; and Mrs. Todd nodded reassuringly and kept to her steady plod, not quickening her gait even when we saw William come round the corner of the house as if to look for us, and wave his hand and disappear.

'Why, William's right on deck; I didn't know's we should see any more of him!' exclaimed Mrs. Todd. 'Now mother'll put the kettle right on; she's got a good fire goin'.' I too could see the blue smoke thicken, and then we both walked a little faster, while Mrs. Todd groped in her full bag of herbs to find the daguerreotypes and be ready to put them in their places.

CHAPTER ELEVEN

The Old Singers

*

WILLIAM was sitting on the side door step, and the old mother was busy making her tea; she gave into my hand an old flowered-glass tea-caddy.

'William thought you'd like to see this, when he was settin' the table. My father brought it to my mother from the island of Tobago; an' here's a pair of beautiful mugs that came with it.' She opened the glass door of a little cupboard beside the chimney. 'These I call my best things, dear,' she said. 'You'd laugh to see how we enjoy 'em Sunday nights in winter: we have a real company tea 'stead o' livin' right along just the same, an' I make somethin' good for a s'prise an' put on some o' my preserves, an' we get a-talkin' together an' have real pleasant times.'

Mrs. Todd laughed indulgently, and looked to see what I thought of such childishness.

'I wish I could be here some Sunday evening,' said I.

'William an' me'll be talkin' about you an' thinkin' o' this nice day,' said Mrs. Blackett affectionately, and she glanced at William, and he looked up bravely and nodded. I began to discover that he and his sister could not speak their deeper feelings before each other.

'Now I want you an' mother to sing,' said Mrs. Todd abruptly, with an air of command, and I gave William much sympathy in his evident distress.

'After I've had my cup o' tea, dear,' answered the old hostess cheerfully; and so we sat down and took our cups and made merry while they lasted. It was impossible not to wish to stay on forever at Green Island, and I could not help saying so.

'I'm very happy here, both winter an' summer,' said old Mrs. Blackett. 'William an' I never wish for any other home, do we, William? I'm glad you find it pleasant; I wish you'd come an' stay, dear, whenever you feel inclined. But here's Almiry; I always think Providence was kind to plot an' have her husband leave her a good house where she really belonged. She'd been very restless if she'd had to continue here on Green Island. You wanted more scope, didn't you, you, Almiry, an' to live in a large place where more things grew? Sometimes folks wonders that we don't live together; perhaps we shall some time,' and a shadow of sadness and apprehension flitted across her face. 'The time o' sickness an' failin' has got to come to all. But Almiry's got an herb that's good for everything.' She smiled as she spoke, and looked bright again.

'There's some herb that's good for everybody, except for them that thinks they're sick when they ain't,' announced Mrs. Todd, with a truly professional air of finality. 'Come, William, let's have Sweet Home, an' then mother'll sing Cupid an' the Bee for us.'

Then followed a most charming surprise. William mastered his timidity and began to sing. His voice was a little faint and frail, like the family daguerreotypes, but it was a tenor voice, and perfectly true and sweet. I have never heard Home, Sweet Home sung as touchingly and seriously as he sang it; he seemed to make it quite new and when he paused for a moment at the end of the first line and began the next, the old mother joined him and they sang together, she missing only the higher notes, where he seemed to lend his voice to hers for the moment and carry on her very note and air. It was the silent man's real and only means of expressing, and one could have listened forever, and have asked for more and more songs of old Scotch and English inheritance and the best that have lived from the ballad music of the war. Mrs. Todd kept time visibly, and sometimes audibly, with her ample foot. I saw the tears in her eyes sometimes, when I could see beyond the tears in mine. But at last the songs ended and the time came to say good-bye; it was the end of a great pleasure.

Mrs. Blackett, the dear old lady, opened the door of her bedroom while Mrs. Todd was tying up the herb bag, and William had gone down to get the boat ready and to blow the horn for Johnny Bowden, who had joined a roving boat party who were off the shore lobstering.

I went to the door of the bedroom, and thought how pleasant it looked, with its pink-and-white patchwork quilt and the brown unpainted panelling of its woodwork.

'Come right in, dear,' she said. 'I want you to set

down in my old quilted rockin'-chair there by the window; you'll say it's the prettiest view in the house. I set there a good deal to rest me and when I want to read.'

There was a worn red Bible on the light-stand, and Mrs. Blackett's heavy silver-bowed glasses; her thimble was on the narrow window-ledge, and folded carefully on the table was a thick striped-cotton shirt that she was making for her son. Those dear old fingers and their loving stitches, that heart which had made the most of everything that needed love! Here was the real home, the heart of the old house on Green Island! I sat in the rocking-chair, and felt that it was a place of peace, the little brown bedroom, and the quiet outlook upon field and sea and sky.

I looked up, and we understood each other without speaking. 'I shall like to think o' your settin' here to-day,' said Mrs. Blackett. 'I want you to come again. It has been so pleasant for William.'

The wind served us all the way home, and did not fall or let the sail slacken until we were close to the shore. We had a generous freight of lobsters in the boat, and new potatoes which William had put aboard, and what Mrs. Todd proudly called a full 'kag' of prime number one salted mackerel; and when we landed we had to make business arrangements to have these conveyed to her house in a wheelbarrow.

I never shall forget the day at Green Island. The town of Dunnet Landing seemed large and noisy and oppressive as we came ashore. Such is the power of contrast; for the village was so still that I could hear the shy whippoorwills singing that night as I lay awake in my downstairs bedroom, and the scent of Mrs. Todd's herb garden under the window blew in again and again with every gentle rising of the sea-breeze.

CHAPTER TWELVE

A Strange Sail

★

EXCEPT for a few stray guests, islanders or from the
inland country, to whom Mrs. Todd offered the
hospitalities of a single meal, we were quite by ourselves all summer; and when there were signs of in-
vasion, late in July, and a certain Mrs. Fosdick appeared like a strange sail on the far horizon, I suffered
much from apprehension. I had been living in the
quaint little house with as much comfort and unconsciousness as if it were a larger body, or a double shell,
in whose simple convolutions Mrs. Todd and I had
secreted ourselves, until some wandering hermit crab
of a visitor marked the little spare room for her own.
Perhaps now and then a castaway on a lonely desert
island dreads the thought of being rescued. I heard of
Mrs. Fosdick for the first time with a selfish sense of
objection; but after all, I was still vacation-tenant of
the school-house, where I could always be alone and
it was impossible not to sympathise with Mrs. Todd,
who, in spite of some preliminary grumbling, was really
delighted with the prospect of entertaining an old friend.

For nearly a month we received occasional news of
Mrs. Fosdick, who seemed to be making a royal progress from house to house in the inland neighbourhood,
after the fashion of Queen Elizabeth. One Sunday
after another came and went, disappointing Mrs.

Todd in the hope of seeing her guest at church and fixing the day for the great visit to begin; but Mrs. Fosdick was not ready to commit herself to a date. An assurance of 'some time this week' was not sufficiently definite from a free-footed house-keeper's point of view, and Mrs. Todd put aside all herb-gathering plans, and went through the various stages of expectation, provocation, and despair. At last she was ready to believe that Mrs. Fosdick must have forgotten her promise and returned to her home, which was vaguely said to be over Thomaston way. But one evening, just as the supper-table was cleared and 'readied up,' and Mrs. Todd had put her large apron over her head and stepped forth for an evening stroll in the garden, the unexpected happened. She heard the sound of wheels, and gave an excited cry to me, as I sat by the window, that Mrs. Fosdick was coming right up the street.

'She may not be considerate, but she's dreadful good company,' said Mrs. Todd hastily, coming back a few steps from the neighbourhood of the gate. 'No, she ain't a mite considerate, but there's a small lobster left over from your tea; yes, it's a real mercy there's a lobster. Susan Fosdick might just as well have passed the compliment o' comin' an hour ago.'

'Perhaps she has had her supper,' I ventured to suggest, sharing the house-keeper's anxiety, and meekly conscious of an inconsiderate appetite for my own supper after a long expedition up the bay. There were so few emergencies of any sort at Dunnet Landing that this one appeared overwhelming.

'No, she's rode 'way over from Nahum Brayton's place. I expect they were busy on the farm, and couldn't spare the horse in proper season. You just sly out an' set the teakittle on again, dear, an' drop in a good han'ful o' chips; the fire's all alive. I'll take her right up to lay off her things, an' she'll be occupied with explanations an' gettin' her bunnit off, so you'll have plenty o' time. She's one I shouldn't like to have find me unprepared.'

Mrs. Fosdick was already at the gate, and Mrs. Todd now turned with an air of complete surprise and delight to welcome her.

'Why, Susan Fosdick,' I heard her exclaim in a fine unhindered voice, as if she were calling across a field, 'I come near giving of you up! I was afraid you'd gone an' 'portioned out my visit to somebody else. I s'pose you've been to supper?'

'Lor', no, I ain't, Almiry Todd,' said Mrs. Fosdick cheerfully, as she turned, laden with bags and bundles, from making her adieux to the boy driver. 'I ain't had a mite o' supper, dear. I've been lottin' all the way on a cup o' that best tea o' yourn, – some o' that Oolong you keep in the little chist. I don't want none o' your useful herbs.'

'I keep that tea for ministers' folks,' gaily responded Mrs. Todd. 'Come right along, in, Susan Fosdick. I declare if you ain't the same old sixpence!'

As they came up the walk together, laughing like girls, I fled, full of cares, to the kitchen, to brighten the fire and be sure that the lobster, sole dependence of a late supper, was well out of reach of the cat. There proved to be fine reserves of wild raspberries and bread and butter, so that I regained my composure, and waited impatiently for my own share of this illustrious visit to begin. There was an instant sense of high festivity in the evening air from the moment when our guest had so frankly demanded the Oolong tea.

The great moment arrived. I was formally presented at the stair-foot, and the two friends passed on to the kitchen, where I soon heard a hospitable clink of crockery and the brisk stirring of a tea-cup. I sat in my high-backed rocking-chair by the window in the front room with an unreasonable feeling of being left out, like the child who stood at the gate in Hans Andersen's story. Mrs. Fosdick did not look, at first sight, like a person of great social gifts. She was a serious-looking little bit of an old woman, with a birdlike nod of the head. I had often been told that she was the 'best hand in the world to make a visit,' — as if to visit were the highest of vocations; that everybody wished for her, while few could get her; and I saw that Mrs. Todd felt a comfortable sense of distinction in being favoured with the company of this eminent person who 'knew just how.' It was certainly true that Mrs. Fosdick gave both her hostess and me a warm feeling of enjoyment and expectation, as if she had the power of social suggestion to all neighbouring minds.

The two friends did not reappear for at least an hour I could hear their busy voices, loud and low by turns, as they ranged from public to confidential topics. At last Mrs. Todd kindly remembered me and returned, giving my door a ceremonious knock before she stepped in, with the small visitor in her wake. She reached behind her and took Mrs. Fosdick's hand as if she were young and bashful, and gave her a gentle pull forward.

'There, I don't know whether you're goin' to take to each other or not; no, nobody can't tell whether you'll suit each other, but I expect you'll get along some way, both having seen the world,' said our affectionate hostess. 'You can inform Mis' Fosdick how we found the folks out to Green Island the other day. She's always been well acquainted with mother. I'll slip out now an' put away the supper things an' set my bread to rise, if you'll both excuse me. You can come out an' keep me company when you get ready, either or both.' And Mrs. Todd, large and amiable, disappeared and left us.

Being furnished not only with a subject of conversation, but with a safe refuge in the kitchen in case of incompatibility, Mrs. Fosdick and I sat down, prepared to make the best of each other. I soon discovered that she, like many of the elder women of that coast, had spent a part of her life at sea, and was full of a good traveller's curiosity and enlightenment. By the time we thought it discreet to join our hostess we were already sincere friends.

You may speak of a visit's setting in as well as a tide's, and it was impossible, as Mrs. Todd whispered to me, not to be pleased at the way this visit was setting in; a new impulse and refreshing of the social currents and seldom visited bays of memory appeared to have begun. Mrs. Fosdick had been the mother of a large family of sons and daughters, – sailors and sailors' wives, – and most of them had died before her. I soon grew more or less acquainted with the histories of all their fortunes and misfortunes, and subjects of an intimate nature were no more withheld from my ears than if I had been a shell on the mantelpiece. Mrs. Fosdick was not without a touch of dignity and elegance; she was fashionable in her dress, but it was a curiously well-preserved provincial fashion of some years back. In a wider sphere one might have called her a woman of the world, with her unexpected bits of modern knowledge, but Mrs. Todd's wisdom was an intimation of truth itself. She might belong to any age, like an idyl of Theocritus; but while she always understood Mrs. Fosdick, that entertaining pilgrim could not always understand Mrs. Todd.

That very first evening my friends plunged into a borderless sea of reminiscences and personal news. Mrs. Fosdick had been staying with a family who owned the farm where she was born, and she had visited every sunny knoll and shady field corner; but when she said that it might be for the last time, I detected in her tone something expectant of the contradiction which Mrs. Todd promptly offered.

'Almiry,' said Mrs. Fosdick, with sadness, 'you may say what you like, but I am one of nine brothers and sisters brought up on the old place, and we're all dead but me.'

'Your sister Dailey ain't gone, is she? Why, no, Louisa ain't gone!' exclaimed Mrs. Todd, with surprise. 'Why, I never heard of that occurrence!'

'Yes'm; she passed away last October, in Lynn. She had made her distant home in Vermont State, but she was making a visit to her youngest daughter. Louisa was the only one of my family whose funeral I wasn't able to attend, but 't was a mere accident. All the rest of us were settled right about home. I thought it was very slack of 'em in Lynn not to fetch her to the old place; but when I came to hear about it, I learned that they'd recently put up a very elegant monument, and my sister Dailey was always great for show. She'd just been out to see the monument the week before she was taken down, and admired it so much that they felt sure of her wishes.'

'So she's really gone, and the funeral was up to Lynn!' repeated Mrs. Todd, as if to impress the sad fact upon her mind. 'She was some years younger than we be too. I recollect the first day she ever came to school; 't was that first year mother sent me inshore to

stay with Aunt Topham's folks and get my schooling.
You fetched little Louisa to school one Monday
mornin' in a pink dress an' her long curls, and she set
between you an' me, and got cryin' after a while, so
the teacher sent us home with her at recess.'

'She was scared of seeing so many children about her;
there was only her and me and brother John at home
then; the older boys were to sea with father, an' the
rest of us wa'n't born,' explained Mrs. Fosdick. 'That
next fall we all went to sea together. Mother was uncertain till the last minute, as one may say. The ship
was waiting orders, but the baby that then was, was
born just in time, and there was a long spell of extra
bad weather, so mother got about again before they had
to sail, an' we all went. I remember my clothes were
all left ashore in the east chamber in a basket where
mother'd took them out o' my chist o' drawers an' left
'em ready to carry aboard. She didn't have nothing
aboard of her own that she wanted to cut up for me, so
when my dress wore out she just put me into a spare
suit o' John's, jacket and trousers. I wasn't but eight
years old an' he was most seven and large of his age.
Quick as we made a port she went right ashore an'
fitted me out pretty, but we was bound for the East
Indies and didn't put in anywhere for a good while. So
I had quite a spell o' freedom. Mother made my new
skirt long because I was growing, and I poked about the
deck after that, real discouraged, feeling the hem at my
heels every minute, and as if youth was past and gone.

I liked the trousers best; I used to climb the riggin' with 'em and frighten mother till she said an' vowed she'd never take me to sea again.'

I thought by the polite absent-minded smile on Mrs. Todd's face this was no new story.

'Little Louisa was a beautiful child; yes, I always thought Louisa was very pretty,' Mrs. Todd said. 'She was a dear little girl in those days. She favoured your mother; the rest of you took after your father's folks.'

'We did certain,' agreed Mrs. Fosdick, rocking steadily. 'There, it does seem so pleasant to talk with an old acquaintance that knows what you know. I see so many of these new folks nowadays, that seem to have neither past nor future. Conversation's got to have some root in the past, or else you've got to explain every remark you make, an' it wears a person out.'

Mrs. Todd gave a funny little laugh. 'Yes'm, old friends is always best, 'less you can catch a new one that's fit to make an old one out of,' she said, and we gave an affectionate glance at each other, which Mrs. Fosdick could not have understood, being the latest comer to the house.

CHAPTER THIRTEEN

Poor Joanna

*

ONE evening my ears caught a mysterious allusion
which Mrs. Todd made to Shell-heap Island. It was a
chilly night of cold north-easterly rain, and I made a
fire for the first time in the Franklin stove in my room,
and begged my two housemates to come in and keep
me company. The weather had convinced Mrs. Todd
that it was time to make a supply of cough-drops, and
she had been bringing forth herbs from dark and dry
hiding-places, until now the pungent dust and odour of
them had resolved themselves into one mighty flavour
of spearmint that came from a simmering caldron of
syrup in the kitchen. She called it done, and well done,
and had ostentatiously left it to cool, and taken her
knitting-work because Mrs. Fosdick was busy with hers.
They sat in the two rocking-chairs, the small woman
and the large one, but now and then I could see that
Mrs. Todd's thoughts remained with the cough-drops.
The time of gathering herbs was nearly over, but the
time of syrups and cordials had begun.

The heat of the open fire made us a little drowsy,
but something in the way Mrs. Todd spoke of Shell-
heap Island waked my interest. I waited to see if she
would say any more, and then took a roundabout way
back to the subject by saying what was first in my mind:
that I wished the Green Island family were there to

spend the evening with us, – Mrs. Todd's mother and her brother William.

Mrs. Todd smiled, and drummed on the arm of the rocking-chair. 'Might scare William to death,' she warned me; and Mrs. Fosdick mentioned her intention of going out to Green Island to stay two or three days, if this wind didn't make too much sea.

'Where is Shell-heap Island?' I ventured to ask, seizing the opportunity.

'Bears nor'east somewheres about three miles from Green Island; right off-shore, I should call it about eight miles out,' said Mrs. Todd. 'You never was there, dear; 'tis off the thoroughfares, and a very bad place to land at best.'

'I should think 'twas,' agreed Mrs. Fosdick, smoothing down her black silk apron. ''T is a place worth visitin' when you once get there. Some o' the old folks was kind o' fearful about it. 'Twas 'counted a great place in old Indian times; you can pick up their stone tools 'most any time if you hunt about. There's a beautiful spring o' water, too. Yes, I remember when they used to tell queer stories about Shell-heap Island. Some said 't was a great bangeing-place for the Indians, and an old chief resided there once that ruled the winds; and others said they'd always heard that once the Indians come down from up country an' left a captive there without any bo't, an' 't was too far to swim across to Black Island, so called, an' he lived there till he perished.'

'I've heard say he walked the island after that, and sharp-sighted folks could see him an' lose him like one o' them citizens Cap'n Littlepage was acquainted with up to the north pole,' announced Mrs. Todd grimly. 'Anyway, there was Indians, – you can see their shell-heap that named the island; and I've heard myself that 't was one o' their cannibal places, but I never could believe it. There never was no cannibals on the coast o' Maine. All the Indians o' these regions are tame-looking folks.'

'Sakes alive, yes!' exclaimed Mrs. Fosdick. 'Ought to see them painted savages I've seen when I was young out in the South Sea Islands! That was the time for folks to travel, 'way back in the old whalin' days!'

'Whalin' must have been dull for a lady, hardly ever makin' a lively port, and not takin' in any mixed cargoes,' said Mrs. Todd. 'I never desired to go a whalin' v'y'ge myself.'

'I used to return feelin' very slack an' behind the times, 'tis true,' explained Mrs. Fosdick, 'but 't was excitin', an' we always done extra well, and felt rich when we did get ashore. I liked the variety. There, how times have changed; how few seafarin' families there are left! What a lot o' queer folks there used to be about here, anyway, when we was young, Almiry. Everybody's just like everybody else, now; nobody to laugh about, and nobody to cry about.'

It seemed to me that there were peculiarities of

93

character in the region of Dunnet Landing yet, but I did not like to interrupt.

'Yes,' said Mrs. Todd after a moment of meditation, 'there was certain a good many curiosities of human natur' in this neighbourhood years ago. There was more energy then, and in some the energy took a singular turn. In these days the young folks is all copy-cats, 'fraid to death they won't be all just alike; as for the old folks, they pray for the advantage o' bein' a little different.'

'I ain't heard of a copy-cat this great many years,' said Mrs. Fosdick, laughing; ''t was a favourite term o' my grandmother's. No, I wa'n't thinking o' those things, but of them strange straying creatur's that used to rove the country. You don't see them now, or the ones that used to hive away in their own houses with some strange notion or other.'

I thought again of Captain Littlepage but my companions were not reminded of his name; and there was brother William at Green Island, whom we all three knew.

'I was talking o' poor Joanna the other day. I hadn't thought of her for a great while,' said Mrs. Fosdick abruptly. 'Mis' Brayton an' I recalled her as we sat together sewing. She was one o' your peculiar persons, wa'n't she? Speaking of such persons,' she turned to explain to me, 'there was a sort of a nun or hermit person lived out there for years all alone on Shell-heap Island. Miss Joanna Todd, her name was – a cousin o' Almiry's late husband.'

94

I expressed my interest, but as I glanced at Mrs. Todd I saw that she was confused by sudden affectionate feeling and unmistakable desire for reticence.

'I never want to hear Joanna laughed about,' she said anxiously.

'Nor I,' answered Mrs. Fosdick reassuringly. 'She was crossed in love, – that was all the matter to begin with; but as I look back, I can see that Joanna was one doomed from the first to fall into a melancholy. She retired from the world for good an' all, though she was a well-off woman. All she wanted was to get away from folks; she thought she wasn't fit to live with anybody, and wanted to be free. Shell-heap Island come to her from her father, and first thing folks knew she'd gone off out there to live, and left word she didn't want no company. 'T was a bad place to get to, unless the wind an' tide were just right; 't was hard work to make a landing.'

'What time of year was this?' I asked.

'Very late in the summer,' said Mrs. Fosdick. 'No, I never could laugh at Joanna, as some did. She set everything by the young man, an' they were going to marry in about a month, when he got bewitched with a girl 'way up the bay, and married her, and went off to Massachusetts. He wasn't well thought of, – there were those who thought Joanna's money was what had tempted him; but she'd given him her whole heart, an' she wa'n't so young as she had been. All her hopes were built on marryin', an' havin' a real home and somebody to look to; she acted just like a bird when its nest is spoilt. The day after she heard the news she was in dreadful woe, but the next she came to herself very quiet, and took the horse and waggon, and drove fourteen miles to the lawyer's, and signed a paper givin' her half of the farm to her brother. They never had got along very well together, but he didn't want to sign it, till she acted so distressed that he gave in. Edward Todd's wife was a good woman, who felt very bad indeed, and used every argument with Joanna; but Joanna took a poor old boat that had been her father's and lo'ded in a few things, and off she put all alone, with a good land breeze, right out to sea. Edward Todd ran down to the beach, an' stood there cryin' like a boy to see her go, but she was out o' hearin'. She never stepped foot on the mainland again long as she lived.'

'How large an island is it? How did she manage in winter?' I asked.

'Perhaps thirty acres, rocks and all,' answered Mrs. Todd, taking up the story gravely. 'There can't be much of it that the salt spray don't fly over in storms. No, 't is a dreadful small place to make a world of; it has a different look from any of the other islands, but there's a sheltered cove on the south side, with mud-flats across one end of it at low water where there's excellent clams, and the big shell-heaps keep some o' the wind off a little house her father took the trouble to build when he was a young man. They said there was an old house built o' logs there before that, with a kind of natural cellar in the rock under it. He used to stay out there days to a time, and anchor a little sloop he had, and dig clams to fill it, and sail up to Portland. They said the dealers always gave him an extra price, the clams were so noted. Joanna used to go out and stay with him. They were always great companions, so she knew just what 't was out there. There was a few sheep that belonged to her brother an' her, but she bargained for him to come and get them on the edge o' cold weather. Yes, she desired him to come for the sheep; an' his wife thought perhaps Joanna'd return, but he said no, an' lo'ded the bo't with warm things an' what he thought she'd need through the winter. He come home with the sheep an' left the other things by the house, but she never so much as looked out o' the window. She done it for a penance. She must have wanted to see Edward by that time.'

Mrs. Fosdick was fidgeting with eagerness to speak.

'Some thought the first cold snap would set her ashore, but she always remained,' concluded Mrs. Todd soberly.

'Talk about the men not having any curiosity!' exclaimed Mrs. Fosdick scornfully. 'Why, the waters round Shell-heap Island were white with sails all that fall. 'T was never called no great of a fishin'-ground before. Many of 'em made excuse to go ashore to get water at the spring; but at last she spoke to a bo't-load, very dignified and calm, and said that she'd like it better if they'd make a practice of getting water to Black Island or somewheres else and leave her alone, except in case of accident or trouble. But there was one man who had always set everything by her from a boy. He'd have married her if the other hadn't come about an' spoilt his chance, and he used to get close to the island, before light, on his way out fishin', and throw a little bundle 'way up the green slope front o' the house. His sister told me she happened to see, the first time, what a pretty choice he made o' useful things that a woman would feel lost without. He stood off fishin', and could see them in the grass all day, though sometimes she'd come out and walk right by them. There was other bo'ts near, out after mackerel. But early next morning his present was gone. He didn't presume too much, but once he took her a nice firkin o' things he got up to Portland, and when spring come he landed her a hen and chickens in a nice little coop. There was a good many old friends had Joanna on their minds.'

'Yes,' said Mrs. Todd, losing her sad reserve in the growing sympathy of these reminiscences. 'How everybody used to notice whether there was smoke out of the chimney! The Black Island folks could see her with their spy-glass, and if they'd ever missed getting some sign o' life they'd have sent notice to her folks. But after the first year or two Joanna was more and more forgotten as an everyday charge. Folks lived very simple in those days, you know,' she continued, as Mrs. Fosdick's knitting was taking much thought at the moment. 'I expect there was always plenty of driftwood thrown up, and a poor failin' patch of spruces covered all the north side of the island, so she always had something to burn. She was very fond of workin' in the garden ashore, and that first summer she began to till the little field out there, and raised a nice parcel o' potatoes. She could fish, o' course, and there was all her clams an' lobsters. You can always live well in any wild place by the sea when you'd starve to death up country, except 'twas berry time. Joanna had berries out there, blackberries at least, and there was a few herbs in case she needed them. Mullein in great quantities and a plant o' wormwood, I remember seeing once when I stayed there, long before she fled out to Shell-heap. Yes, I recall the wormwood, which is is always a planted herb, so there must have been folks there before the Todds' day. A growin' bush makes the best gravestone; I expect that wormwood always stood for somebody's solemn monument. Catnip, too, is a very endurin' herb about an old place.'

'But what I want to know is what she did for other things,' interrupted Mrs. Fosdick. 'Almiry, what did she do for clothin' when she needed to replenish, or risin' for her bread, or the piece-bag that no woman can live long without?'

'Or company,' suggested Mrs. Todd. 'Joanna was one that loved her friends. There must have been a terrible sight o' long winter evenin's that first year.'

'There was her hens,' suggested Mrs. Fosdick, after

reviewing the melancholy situation. 'She never wanted the sheep after that first season. There wa'n't no proper pasture for sheep after the June grass was past, and she ascertained the fact and couldn't bear to see them suffer; but the chickens done well. I remember sailin' by one spring afternoon, an' seein' the coops out front o' the house in the sun. How long was it before you went out with the minister? You were the first ones that ever really got ashore to see Joanna.'

I had been reflecting upon a state of society which admitted such personal freedom and a voluntary hermitage. There was something medieval in the behaviour of poor Joanna Todd under a disappointment of the heart. The two women had drawn closer together, and were talking on, quite unconscious of a listener.

'Poor Joanna!' said Mrs. Todd again, and sadly shook her head as if there were things one could not speak about.

'I called her a great fool,' declared Mrs. Fosdick, with spirit, 'but I pitied her then, and I pity her far more now. Some other minister would have been a great help to her, – one that preached self-forgetfulness and goin' for others to cure our own ills; but Parson Dimmick was a vague person, well meanin', but very numb in his feelin's. I don't suppose at that troubled time Joanna could think of any way to mend her troubles except to run off and hide.'

'Mother used to say she didn't see how Joanna lived

without having nobody to do for, getting her own meals and tending her own poor self day in an' day out,' said Mrs. Todd sorrowfully.

'There was the hens,' repeated Mrs. Fosdick kindly. 'I expect she soon came to makin' folks o' them. No, I never went to work to blame Joanna, as some did. She was full o' feeling, and her troubles hurt her more than she could bear. I see it all now as I couldn't when I was young.'

'I suppose in old times they had their shut-up convents for just such folks,' said Mrs. Todd, as if she and her friend had disagreed about Joanna once, and were now in happy harmony. She seemed to speak with new openness and freedom. 'Oh, yes, I was only too pleased when the Reverend Dimmick invited me to go out with him. He hadn't been very long in the place when Joanna left home and friends. 'T was one day that next summer after she went, and I had been married early in the spring. He felt that he ought to go out and visit her. She was a member of the church, and might wish to have him consider her spiritual state. I wa'n't so sure o' that, but I always liked Joanna, and I'd come to be her cousin by marriage. Nathan an' I had conversed about goin' out to pay her a visit, but he got his chance to sail sooner'n he expected. He always thought everything of her, and last time he come home, knowing nothing of her change, he brought her a beautiful coral pin from a port he'd touched at somewheres up the Mediterranean. So I wrapped the little box in a nice piece of paper and put it in my pocket, and picked her a bunch of fresh lemon balm, and off we started.'

Mrs. Fosdick laughed. 'I remember hearin' about your trials on the v'y'ge,' she said.

'Why, yes,' continued Mrs. Todd in her company manner. 'I picked her the balm, an' we started. Why, yes, Susan, the minister liked to have cost me my life that day. He would fasten the sheet, though I advised against it. He said the rope was rough an' cut his hand. There was a fresh breeze, an' he went on talking rather high flown, an' I felt some interested. All of a sudden there come up a gust, and he gave a screech and stood right up and called for help, 'way out there to sea. I knocked him right over into the bottom o' the bo't, getting by to catch hold of the sheet an' untie it. He wasn't but a little man; I helped him right up after the squall passed, and made a handsome apology to him, but he did act kind o' offended.'

'I do think they ought not to settle them landlocked folks in parishes where they're liable to be on the water,' insisted Mrs. Fosdick. 'Think of the families in our parish that was scattered all about the bay, and what a sight o' sails you used to see, in Mr. Dimmick's day, standing across to the mainland on a pleasant Sunday morning, filled with church-going folks, all sure to want him some time or other! You couldn't find no doctor that would stand up in the boat and screech if a flaw struck her.'

'Old Dr. Bennett had a beautiful sail-boat, didn't he?'

responded Mrs. Todd. 'And how well he used to brave the weather! Mother always said that in time o' trouble that tall white sail used to look like an angel's wing comin' over the sea to them that was in pain. Well, there's a difference in gifts. Mr. Dimmick was not without light.'

"T was light o' the moon,' snapped Mrs. Fosdick; 'he was pompous enough, but I never could remember a single word he said. There, go on, Mis' Todd; I forget a great deal about that day you went to see poor Joanna.'

'I felt she saw us coming, and knew us a great way off; yes, I seemed to feel it within me,' said our friend, laying down her knitting. 'I kept my seat, and took the bo't inshore without saying a word; there was a short channel that I was sure Mr. Dimmick wasn't acquainted with, and the tide was very low. She never came out to warn us off nor anything, and I thought, as I hauled the bo't up on a wave and let the Reverend Mr. Dimmick step out, that it was somethin' gained to be safe ashore. There was a little smoke out o' the chimney o' Joanna's house, and it did look sort of homelike and pleasant with wild mornin'-glory vines trained up; an' there was a plot o' flowers under the front window, portulacas and things. I believe she'd made a garden once, when she was stopping there with her father, and some things must have seeded in. It looked as if she might have gone over to the other side of the island. 'T was neat and pretty all about the house, and a lovely day in July. We walked up from the beach together very sedate, and I felt for poor Nathan's little pin to see if 't was safe in my dress pocket. All of a sudden Joanna come right to the fore door and stood there, not sayin' a word.'

CHAPTER FOURTEEN

The Hermitage

*

My companions and I had been so intent upon the subject of the conversation that we had not heard anyone open the gate, but at this moment, above the noise of the rain, we heard a loud knocking. We were all startled as we sat by the fire, and Mrs. Todd rose hastily and went to answer the call, leaving her rocking-chair in violent motion. Mrs. Fosdick and I heard an anxious voice at the door speaking of a sick child, and Mrs. Todd's kind, motherly voice inviting the messenger in: then we waited in silence. There was a sound of heavy dropping of rain from the eaves, and the distant roar and undertone of the sea. My thoughts flew back to the lonely woman on her outer island; what separation from humankind she must have felt, what terror and sadness, even in a summer storm like this!

'You send right after the doctor if she ain't better in half an hour,' said Mrs. Todd to her worried customer as they parted; and I felt a warm sense of comfort in the evident resources of even so small neighbourhood, but for the poor hermit Joanna there was no neighbour on a winter night.

'How did she look?' demanded Mrs. Fosdick, without preface, as our large hostess returned to the little room with a mist about her from standing long in the wet doorway, and the sudden draught of her coming beat out the smoke and flame from the Franklin stove. 'How did poor Joanna look?'

'She was the same as ever, except I thought she looked smaller,' answered Mrs. Todd after thinking a moment; perhaps it was only a last considering thought about her patient. 'Yes, she was just the same, and looked very nice, Joanna did. I had been married since she left home, an' she treated me like her own folks. I expected she'd look strange, with her hair turned gray in a night or somethin', but she wore a pretty gingham dress I'd often seen her wear before she went away; she must have kept it nice for best in the afternoons. She always had beautiful quiet manners. I remember she waited till we were close to her, and then kissed me real affectionate, and inquired for Nathan before she shook hands with the minister, and then she invited us both in. 'T was the same little house her father had built him when he was a bachelor, with one livin'-room, and a little mite of a bedroom out of it where she slept, but 't was neat as a ship's cabin. There was some old chairs, an' a seat made of a long box that might have held boat tackle an' things to lock up in his fishin' days, and a good enough stove so anybody could cook and keep warm in cold weather. I went over once from home and stayed 'most a week with Joanna when we was girls, and those young happy days rose up before me. Her father was busy all day fishin' or clammin'; he was one o' the pleasantest men in the world, but Joanna's mother had the grim streak, and never knew what it was to be happy. The first minute my eyes fell upon Joanna's face that day I saw how she had grown to look like Mis' Todd. 'T was the mother right over again.'

'Oh, dear me!' said Mrs. Fosdick.

'Joanna had done one thing very pretty. There was a little piece o' swamp on the island where good rushes grew plenty, and she'd gathered 'em, and braided some beautiful mats for the floor and a thick cushion for the long bunk. She'd showed a good deal of invention; you see there was a nice chance to pick up pieces o' wood and boards that drove ashore, and she'd made good use o' what she found. There wasn't no clock, but she had a few dishes on a shelf, and flowers set about in shells fixed to the walls, so it did look sort of homelike, though so lonely and poor. I couldn't keep the tears out o' my eyes, I felt so sad. I said to myself, I must get mother to come over an' see Joanna; the love in mother's heart would warm her, an' she might be able to advise.'

'Oh, no, Joanna was dreadful stern,' said Mrs. Fosdick.

'We were all settin' down very proper, but Joanna would keep stealin' glances at me as if she was glad I come. She had but little to say; she was real polite an' gentle, and yet forbiddin'. The minister found it hard,' confessed Mrs. Todd; 'he got embarrassed, an' when he put on his authority and asked her if she felt to enjoy religion in her present situation, an' she replied that she must be excused from answerin', I thought I should fly. She might have made it easier for him; after all, he was the minister and had taken some trouble to come out, though 't was kind of cold an' un-feelin' the way he inquired. I thought he might have seen the little old Bible a-layin' on the shelf close by him, an' I wished he knew enough to just lay his hand on it an' read somethin' kind an' fatherly 'stead of accusin' her, an' then given poor Joanna his blessin' with the hope she might be led to comfort. He did offer prayer, but 't was all about hearin' the voice o' God out o' the whirlwind; and I thought while he was goin' on that anybody that had spent the long cold winter all alone out on Shell-heap Island knew a good deal more about those things than he did. I got so provoked I opened my eyes and stared right at him.

'She didn't take no notice, she kep' a nice respectful manner towards him, and when there come a pause she asked if he had any interest about the old Indian remains, and took down some queer stone gouges and hammers off of one of her shelves and showed them to him same's if he was a boy. He remarked that he'd like to walk over an' see the shell-heap; so she went right to the door and pointed him the way. I see then that she'd made her some kind o' sandal-shoes out o' the fine rushes to wear on her feet; she stepped light an' nice in 'em as shoes.'

Mrs. Fosdick leaned back in her rocking-chair and gave a heavy sigh.

'I didn't move at first, but I'd held out just as long

as I could,' said Mrs. Todd, whose voice trembled a little.
'When Joanna returned from the door, an' I could see
that man's stupid back departin' among the wild rose
bushes, I just ran to her an' caught her in my arms.
I wasn't so big as I be now, and she was older than me,
but I hugged her tight, just as if she was a child. "Oh,
Joanna dear," I says, "won't you come ashore an' live
'long o' me at the Landin', or go over to Green Island
to mother's when winter comes? Nobody shall trouble
you, an' mother finds it hard bein' alone. I can't bear
to leave you here" – and I burst right out crying. I'd
had my own trials, young as I was, an' she knew it.
Oh, I did entreat her; yes, I entreated Joanna.'

'What did she say then?' asked Mrs. Fosdick, much
moved.

'She looked the same way, sad an' remote through it
all,' said Mrs. Todd mournfully. 'She took hold of my
hand, and we sat down close together; 't was as if she
turned round an' made a child of me. "I haven't got
no right to live with folks no more," she said. "You
must never ask me again, Almiry: I've done the only
thing I could do, and I've made my choice. I feel a
great comfort in your kindness, but I don't deserve it.
I have committed the unpardonable sin; you don't
understand," says she humbly. "I was in great wrath
and trouble, and my thoughts was so wicked towards
God that I can't expect to be forgiven. I have come to
know what it is to have patience, but I have lost my hope.
You must tell those that ask how 't is with me," she

said, "an' tell them I want to be alone." I couldn't speak; no, there wa'n't anything I could say, she seemed so above everything common. I was a good deal younger then than I be now, and I got Nathan's little coral pin out o' my pocket and put it into her hand; and when she saw and I told her where it come from, her face did really light up for a minute, sort of bright an' pleasant. "Nathan an' I was always good friends; I'm glad he don't think hard of me," says she. "I want you to have it, Almiry, an' wear it for love o' both o' us," and she handed it back to me. "You give my love to Nathan, – he's a dear good man," she said; "an' tell your mother, if I should be sick she mustn't wish I could get well, but I want her to be the one to come." Then she seemed to have said all she wanted to, as if she was done with the world, and we sat there a few minutes longer together. It was real sweet and quiet except for a good many birds and the sea rollin' up on the beach; but at last she rose, an' I did too, and she kissed me and held my hand in hers a minute, as if to say good-bye; then she turned and went right away out o' the door and disappeared.

'The minister come back pretty soon, and I told him I was all ready, and we started down to the bo't. He had picked up some round stones and things and was carrying them in his pocket-handkerchief; an' he sat down amidships without making any question, and let me take the rudder an' work the bo't, an' made no remarks for some time, until we sort of eased it off speaking of the weather, an' subjects that arose as we skirted Black Island, where two or three families lived belongin' to the parish. He preached next Sabbath as usual, somethin' high soundin' about the creation, and I couldn't help thinkin' he might never get no further; he seemed to know no remedies, but he had a great use of words.'

Mrs. Fosdick sighed again. 'Hearin' you tell about Joanna brings the time right back as if 't was yesterday,' she said. 'Yes, she was one o' them poor things that talked about the great sin; we don't seem to hear nothing about the unpardonable sin now, but you may say 't was not uncommon then.'

'I expect that if it had been in these days, such a person would be plagued to death with idle folks,' continued Mrs. Todd, after a long pause. 'As it was, nobody trespassed on her; all the folks about the bay respected her an' her feelings; but as time wore on, after you left here, one after another ventured to make occasion to put somethin' ashore for her if they went that way. I know mother used to go to see her sometimes, and send William over now and then with something fresh an' nice from the farm. There is a point on the sheltered side where you can lay a boat close to shore an' land anything safe on the turf out o' reach o' the water. There were one or two others, old folks, that she would see, and now an' then she'd hail a passin' boat an' ask for somethin'; and mother got her to promise that she would make some sign to the Black Island folks if she wanted help. I never saw her myself to speak to after that day.'

'I expect nowadays, if such a thing happened, she'd have gone out West to her uncle's folks or up to Massachusetts and had a change, an' come home good as new. The world's bigger an' freer than it used to be,' urged Mrs. Fosdick.

'No,' said her friend. "T is like bad eyesight, the mind of such a person: if your eyes don't see right there may be a remedy, but there's no kind of glasses to remedy the mind. No, Joanna was Joanna, and there she lays on her island where she lived and did her poor penance. She told mother the day she was dyin' that she always used to want to be fetched inshore when it come to the last; but she'd thought it over, and desired to be laid on the island, if 't was thought right. So the funeral was out there, a Saturday afternoon in September. 'T was a pretty day, and there wa'n't hardly a boat on the coast within twenty miles that didn't head for Shell-heap cramfull o' folks, an' all real respectful, same's if she'd always stayed ashore and held her friends. Some went out o' mere curiosity, I don't doubt, – there's always such to every funeral; but most had real feelin', and went purpose to show it. She'd got most o' the wild sparrows as tame as could be, livin' out there so long among 'em, and one flew right in and lit on the coffin an' begun to sing while Mr. Dimmick was speakin'. He was put out by it, an' acted as if he didn't know whether to stop or go on. I may have been prejudiced, but I wa'n't the only one thought the poor little bird done the best of the two.'

'What became o' the man that treated her so, did you ever hear?' asked Mrs. Fosdick. 'I know he lived up to Massachusetts for a while. Somebody who came from the same place told me that he was in trade there an' doin' very well, but that was years ago.'

'I never heard anything more than that; he went to the war in one o' the early rigiments. No, I never heard any more of him,' answered Mrs. Todd. 'Joanna was another sort of person, and perhaps he showed good judgment in marryin' somebody else, if only he'd behaved straightforward and manly. He was a shifty-eyed, coaxin' sort of man, that got what he wanted out o' folks, an' only gave when he wanted to buy, made friends easy and lost 'em without knowin' the difference. She'd had a piece o' work tryin' to make him walk accordin' to her right ideas, but she'd have had too much variety ever to fall into a melancholy. Some is meant to be the Joannas in this world, an' 't was her poor lot.'

CHAPTER FIFTEEN

On Shell-Heap Island

*

SOME time after Mrs. Fosdick's visit was over and we had returned to our former quietness, I was out sailing alone with Captain Bowden in his large boat. We were taking the crooked north-easterly channel seaward, and were well out from shore while it was still early in the afternoon. I found myself presently among some unfamiliar islands, and suddenly remembered the story of poor Joanna. There is something in the fact of a hermitage that cannot fail to touch the imagination; the recluses are a sad kindred, but they are never commonplace. Mrs. Todd had truly said that Joanna was like one of the saints in the desert; the loneliness of sorrow will forever keep alive their sad succession.

'Where is Shell-heap Island!' I asked eagerly.

'You see Shell-heap now, layin' 'way out beyond Black Island there,' answered the captain, pointing with outstretched arm as he stood, and holding the rudder with his knee.

'I should like very much to go there,' said I, and the captain, without comment, changed his course a little more to the eastward and let the reef out of his mainsail.

'I don't know's we can make an easy landin' for ye,' he remarked doubtfully. 'May get your feet wet; bad place to land. Trouble is I ought to have brought a tag-boat; but they clutch on to the water so, an' I do love to sail free. This gr'et boat gets easy bothered with anything trailin'. 'T ain't breaking' much on the meetin'-house ledges; guess I can fetch in to Shell-heap.'

'How long is it since Miss Joanna Todd died?' I asked, partly by way of explanation.

'Twenty-two years come September,' answered the captain, after reflection. 'She died the same year my oldest boy was born, an' the town house was burnt over to the Port. I didn't know but you merely wanted to hunt for some o' them Indian relics. Long's you want to see where Joanna lived — No, 't ain't breakin' over the ledges; we'll manage to fetch across the shoals somehow, 't is such a distance to go 'way round, and tide's a-risin',' he ended hopefully, and we sailed steadily on, the captain speechless with intent watching of a difficult course, until the small island with its low whitish promontory lay in full view before us under the bright afternoon sun.

The month was August, and I had seen the colour of the islands change from the fresh green of June to a sunburnt brown that made them look like stone, except where the dark green of the spruces and fir balsam kept the tint that even winter storms might deepen, but not fade. The few wind-bent trees on Shell-heap Island were mostly dead and gray, but there were some low-growing bushes, and a stripe of light green ran along just above the shore, which I knew to be wild morning-glories. As we came close I could see the high stone walls of a small square field, though there were no sheep left to assail it; and below, there was a little harbour-like cove where Captain Bowden was boldly running the great boat in to seek a landing-place. There was a crooked channel of deep water which led close up against the shore.

'There, you hold fast for'ard there, an' wait for her to lift on the wave. You'll make a good landin' if you're smart; right on the porthand side!' the captain called excitedly; and I, standing ready with high ambition, seized my chance and leaped over to the grassy bank.

'I'm beat if I ain't aground after all!' mourned the captain despondently.

But I could reach the bowsprit, and he pushed with the boat-hook, while the wind veered round a little as if on purpose and helped with the sail; so presently the boat was free and began to drift out from shore.

'Used to call this p'int Joanna's wharf privilege, but 't has worn away in the weather since her time. I thought one or two bumps wouldn't hurt us none, – paint's got to be renewed, anyway – but I never thought she'd tetch. I figured on shyin' by,' the captain apologised. 'She's too gre't a boat to handle well in here; but I used to sort of shy by in Joanna's day, an' cast a little somethin' ashore – some apples or a couple o' pears if I had 'em – on the grass, where she'd be sure to see.'

I stood watching while Captain Bowden cleverly found his way back to deeper water. 'You needn't make no haste,' he called to me; 'I'll keep within call. Joanna lays right up there in the far corner o' the field. There used to be a path led to the place. I always knew her well. I was out here to the funeral.'

I found the path; it was touching to discover that this lonely spot was not without its pilgrims. Later generations will know less and less of Joanna herself, but there are paths trodden to the shrines of solitude the world over, – the world cannot forget them, try as it may; the feet of the young find them out because of curiosity and dim foreboding, while the old bring hearts full of remembrance. This plain anchorite had been one of those whom sorrow made too lonely to brave the sight of men, too timid to front the simple world she knew, yet valiant enough to live alone with her poor insistent human nature and the calms and passions of the sea and sky.

The birds were flying all about the field; they fluttered up out of the grass at my feet as I walked along, so tame that I liked to think they kept some happy tradition from summer to summer of the safety of nests and good fellowship of mankind. Poor Joanna's house was gone except the stones of its foundations, and there was little trace of her flower garden except a single faded sprig of much-enduring French pinks, which a great bee and a yellow butterfly were befriending together. I drank at the spring, and thought that now and then some would follow me from the busy, hard-worked, and simple-thoughted countryside of the mainland, which lay dim and dreamlike in the August haze, as Joanna must have watched it many a day. There was the world, and here was she with eternity well begun. In the life of each of us, I said to myself, there is a place remote and islanded, and given to endless regret or secret happiness; we are each the uncompanioned hermit and recluse of an hour or a day; we understand our fellows of the cell to whatever age of history they may belong.

But as I stood alone on the island, in the sea-breeze, suddenly there came a sound of distant voices; gay voices and laughter from a pleasure-boat that was going seaward full of boys and girls. I knew, as if she had told me, that poor Joanna must have heard the like on many and many a summer afternoon, and must have welcomed the good cheer in spite of hopelessness and winter weather, and all the sorrow and disappointment in the world.

CHAPTER SIXTEEN

The Great Expedition

✻

Mrs. Todd never by any chance gave warning over night of her great projects and adventures by sea and land. She first came to an understanding with the primal forces of nature, and never trusted to any preliminary promise of good weather, but examined the day for herself in its infancy. Then, if the stars were propitious, and the wind blew from a quarter of good inheritance whence no surprises of sea-turns or southwest sultriness might be feared, long before I was fairly awake, I used to hear a rustle and knocking like a great mouse in the walls, and an impatient tread on the steep garret stairs that led to Mrs. Todd's chief place of storage. She went and came as if she had already started on her expedition with utmost haste and kept returning for something that was forgotten. When I appeared in quest of my breakfast, she would be absent-minded and sparing of speech, as if I had displeased her, and she was now, by main force of principle, holding herself back from altercation and strife of tongues.

These signs of a change became familiar to me in the course of time, and Mrs. Todd hardly noticed some plain proofs of divination one August morning when I said, without preface, that I had just seen the Beggs' best chaise go by, and that we should have to take the grocery. Mrs. Todd was alert in a moment.

'There! I might have known!' she exclaimed. 'It's the 15th of August, when he goes and gets his money. He heired an annuity from an uncle o' his on his mother's side. I understood the uncle said none o' Sam Begg's wife's folks should make free with it, so after Sam's gone it'll all be past an' spent, like last summer. That's what Sam prospers on now, if you can call it prosperin'. Yes, I might have known. 'Tis the 15th o' August with him, an' he gener'ly stops to dinner with a cousin's widow on the way home. Feb'uary an' August is the time. Takes him 'bout all day to go an' come.'

I heard this explanation with interest. The tone of Mrs. Todd's voice was complaining at the last.

'I like the grocery just as well as the chaise,' I hastened to say, referring to a long-bodied high waggon with a canopy-top, like an attenuated four-posted bedstead on wheels, in which we sometimes journeyed. 'We can put things in behind – roots and flowers and raspberries, or anything you are going after – much better than if we had the chaise.'

Mrs. Todd looked stony and unwilling. 'I counted upon the chaise,' she said, turning her back to me, and roughly pushing back all the quiet tumblers on the cup-board shelf as if they had been impertinent. 'Yes, I desired the chaise for once. I ain't goin' berryin' nor to fetch home no more wilted vegetation this year. Season's about past, except for a poor few o' late things,' she added in a milder tone. 'I'm goin' up country. No, I ain't intendin' to go berryin'. I've been plottin' for it the past fortnight and hopin' for a good day.'

'Would you like to have me go too?' I asked frankly, but not without a humble fear that I might have mistaken the purpose of this latest plan.

'Oh, certain, dear!' answered my friend affectionately. 'Oh, no, I never thought o' anyone else for comp'ny, if it's convenient for you, long's poor mother ain't come. I ain't nothin' like so handy with a conveyance as I be with a good bo't. Comes o' my early bringing-up. I expect we've got to make that great waggon do. The tyres want settin' and 'tis all loose-jointed, so I can hear it shackle the other side o' the ridge. We'll put the basket in front. I ain't goin' to have it bouncin' an' twirlin' all the way. Why, I've been makin' some nice hearts and rounds to carry.'

These were signs of high festivity, and my interest deepened moment by moment.

'I'll go down to the Beggs' and get the horse just as soon as I finish my breakfast,' said I. 'Then we can start whenever you are ready.'

Mrs. Todd looked cloudy again. 'I don't know but you look nice enough to go just as you be,' she suggested doubtfully. 'No, you wouldn't want to wear that pretty blue dress o' yourn 'way up country. 'T ain't dusty now, but it may be comin' home. No, I expect you'd rather not wear that and the other hat.'

'Oh, yes. I shouldn't think of wearing these clothes,' said I, with sudden illumination. 'Why, if we're going up country and are likely to see some of your friends, I'll put on my blue dress, and you must wear your watch; I am not going at all if you mean to wear the big hat.'

'Now you're behavin' pretty,' responded Mrs. Todd, with a gay toss of her head and a cheerful smile, as she came across the room, bringing a saucerful of wild raspberries, a pretty piece of salvage from supper-time. 'I was cast down when I see you come to breakfast. I didn't think 'twas just what you'd select to wear to the reunion, where you're goin' to meet everybody.'

'What reunion do you mean?' I asked, not without amazement. 'Not the Bowden Family's? I thought that was going to take place in September.'

'To-day's the day. They sent word the middle o' the week. I thought you might have heard of it. Yes, they changed the day. I been thinkin' we'd talk it over, but you never can tell beforehand how it's goin' to be, but 'taint worth while to wear a day all out before it comes.' Mrs. Todd gave no place to the pleasures of anticipation, but she spoke like the oracle that she was. 'I wish mother was here to go,' she continued sadly. 'I did look for her last night, and I couldn't keep back the tears when the dark really fell and she wa'n't here, she does so enjoy a great occasion. If William had a mite o' snap an' ambition, he'd take the lead at such a time. Mother likes variety, and there ain't but a few nice opportunities 'round her, an' them she has to miss 'less she contrives to get ashore to me. I do re'lly hate to go to the reunion without mother, an' 'tis a beautiful day; every body'll be asking where she is. Once she'd have got here anyway. Poor mother's beginning to feel her age.'

'Why, there's your mother now!' I exclaimed with joy, I was so glad to see the dear old soul again. 'I hear her voice at the gate.' But Mrs. Todd was out of the door before me.

There, sure enough, stood Mrs. Blackett, who must have left Green Island before daylight. She had climbed the steep road from the waterside so eagerly that she was out of breath, and was standing by the garden fence to rest. She held an old-fashioned brown wicker cap-basket in her hand, as if visiting were a thing of everyday, and looked up at us as pleased and triumphant as a child.

'Oh, what a poor, plain garden! Hardly a flower in it except your bush o' balm!' she said. 'But you do keep your garden neat, Almiry. Are you both well, an' goin' up country with me?' She came a step or two closer to meet us, with quaint politeness and quite as delightful as if she were at home. She dropped a quick little curtsey before Mrs. Todd.

'There, mother, what a girl you be! I am so pleased! I was just bewailin' you,' said the daughter, with unwonted feeling. 'I was just bewailin' you, I was so disappointed, an' I kep' myself awake a good piece o' the night scoldin' poor William. I watched for the boat till I was ready to shed tears yisterday, and when 't was comin' dark I kept making errands out to the gate an' down the road to see if you wa'n't in the doldrums somewhere down the bay.'

'There was a head wind, as you know,' said Mrs. Blackett, giving me the cap-basket, and holding my hand affectionately as we walked up the clean-swept path to the door. 'I was partly ready to come, but dear William said I should be all tired out and might get cold, havin' to beat all the way in. So we give it up, and set down and spent the evenin' together. It was a little rough and windy outside, and I guess 't was better judgment; we went to bed very early and made a good start just at daylight. It's been a lovely mornin' on the water. William thought he'd better fetch across beyond Bird Rocks, rowin' the greater part o' the way; then we sailed from there right over to the Landin', makin' only one tack. William'll be in again for me to-morrow, so I can come back here an' rest me over night, an' go to meetin' to-morrow, and have a nice, good visit.'

'She was just havin' her breakfast,' said Mrs. Todd, who had listened eagerly to the long explanation without a word of disapproval, while her face shone more and more with joy. 'You just sit right down an' have a cup of tea and rest you while we make our preparations. Oh, I am so gratified to think you've come! Yes, she was just havin' her breakfast, and we were speakin' of you. Where's William?'

'He went right back; he said he expected some schooners in about noon after bait, but he'll come an' have his dinner with us to-morrow, unless it rains; then next day. I laid his best things out all ready,' explained Mrs. Blackett, a little anxiously. 'This wind will serve him nice all the way home. Yes, I will take a cup of tea, dear, – a cup of tea is always good; and then I'll rest a minute and be all ready to start."

'I do feel condemned for havin' such hard thoughts o' William,' openly confessed Mrs. Todd. She stood before us so large and serious that we both laughed and could not find it in our hearts to convict so rueful a culprit. 'He shall have a good dinner to-morrow, if it can be got, and I shall be real glad to see William,' the confession ended handsomely, while Mrs. Blackett smiled approval and made haste to praise the tea. Then I hurried away to make sure of the grocery waggon. Whatever might be the good of the reunion, I was going to have the pleasure and delight of a day in Mrs. Blackett's company, not to speak of Mrs. Todd's.

The early morning breeze was still blowing, and the warm, sunshiny air was of some ethereal northern sort, with a cool freshness as if it came over new-fallen snow. The world was filled with a fragrance of fir-balsam and the faintest flavour of seaweed from the ledges, bare and brown at low tide in the little harbour. It was so still and so early that the village was but half awake. I could hear no voices but those of the birds, small and great, – the constant song of sparrows, the clink of a yellow-hammer over in the woods, and the far conversation of some deliberate crows. I saw William Blackett's escaping sail already far from land, and

Captain Littlepage was sitting behind his closed window as I passed by, watching for someone who never came. I tried to speak to him, but he did not see me. There was a patient look on the old man's face, as if the world were a great mistake and he had nobody with whom to speak his own language or find companionship.

CHAPTER SEVENTEEN

A Country Road

*

WHATEVER doubts and anxieties I may have had about
the inconvenience of the Beggs' high waggon for a
person of Mrs. Blackett's age and shortness, they were
happily overcome by the aid of a chair and her own
valiant spirit. Mrs. Todd bestowed great care upon
seating us as if we were taking passage by boat, but she
finally pronounced that we were properly trimmed.
When we had gone only a little way up the hill she
remembered that she had left the house door wide open,
though the large key was safe in her pocket. I offered
to run back, but my offer was met with lofty scorn, and
we lightly dismissed the matter from our minds, until
two or three miles further on we met the doctor, and
Mrs. Todd asked him to stop and ask her nearest
neighbour to step over and close the door if the dust
seemed to blow in the afternoon.

'She'll be there in her kitchen; she'll hear you the
minute you call; 't won't give you no delay,' said Mrs.
Todd to the doctor. 'Yes, Mis' Dennett's right there,
with the windows all open. It isn't as if my fore door
opened right on the road, anyway.' At which proof of
composure Mrs. Blackett smiled wisely at me.

The doctor seemed delighted to see our guest; they
were evidently the warmest friends, and I saw a look
of affectionate confidence in their eyes. The good man

left his carriage to speak to us, but as he took Mrs. Blackett's hand he held it a moment, and, as if merely from force of habit, felt her pulse as they talked; then to my delight he gave the firm old wrist a commending pat.

'You're wearing well: good for another ten years at this rate,' he assured her cheerfully, and she smiled back. 'I like to keep a strict account of my old stand-bys,' and he turned to me. 'Don't you let Mrs. Todd overdo to-day, — old folks like her are apt to be thoughtless;' and then we all laughed, and, parting, went our ways gaily.

'I suppose he puts up with your rivalry the same as ever?' asked Mrs. Blackett. 'You and he are 's friendly as ever, I see, Almiry,' and Almira sagely nodded.

'He's got too many long routes now to stop to 'tend to all his door patients,' she said, 'especially them that takes pleasure in talkin' themselves over. The doctor and me have got to be kind of partners; he's gone a good deal, far an' wide. Looked tired, didn't he? I shall have to advise with him an' get him off for a good rest. He'll take the big boat from Rockland an' go off up to Boston an' mouse round among the other doctors, once in two or three years, and come home fresh as a boy. I guess they think consider'ble of him up there.' Mrs. Todd shook the reins and reached determinedly for the whip, as if she were compelling public opinion.

Whatever energy and spirit the white horse had to begin with were soon exhausted by the steep hills and his discernment of a long expedition ahead. We toiled slowly along. Mrs. Blackett and I sat together, and Mrs. Todd sat alone in front with much majesty and the large basket of provisions. Part of the way the road was shaded by thick woods, but we also passed one farmhouse after another on the high uplands, which we all three regarded with deep interest, the house itself and the barns and garden-spots and poultry all having to suffer an inspection of the shrewdest sort. This was a highway quite new to me; in fact, most of my journeys with Mrs. Todd had been made afoot and between the roads, in open pasture lands. My friends stopped several times for brief dooryard visits, and made so many promises of stopping again on the way home that I began to wonder how long the expedition would last. I had often noticed how warmly Mrs. Todd was greeted by her friends, but it was hardly to be compared to the feeling now shown toward Mrs. Blackett. A look of delight came to the faces of those who recognised the plain, dear old figure beside me; one revelation after another was made of the constant interest and inter-course that had linked the far island and these scattered farms into a golden chain of love and dependence.

'Now we mustn't stop again if we can help it,' insisted Mrs. Todd at last. 'You'll get tired, mother, and you'll think the less o' reunions. We can visit along here any day. There, if they ain't frying dough-nuts in this next house, too! These are new folks, you know, from over St. George way; they took this old

Talcot farm last year. 'Tis the best water on the road, and the checkrein's come undone – yes, we'd best delay a little and water the horse.'

We stopped, and seeing a party of pleasure-seekers in holiday attire, the thin, anxious mistress of the farm-house came out with wistful sympathy to hear what news we might have to give. Mrs. Blackett first spied her at the half-closed door, and asked with such cheerful directness if we were trespassing that, after a few words, she went back to her kitchen and reappeared with a plateful of doughnuts.

'Entertainment for man and beast,' announced Mrs. Todd with satisfaction. 'Why, we've perceived there was new doughnuts all along the road, but you're the first that has treated us.'

Our new acquaintance flushed with pleasure, but said nothing.

'They're very nice; you've had good luck with 'em,' pronounced Mrs. Todd. 'Yes, we've observed there was doughnuts all the way along; if one house is frying all the rest is; 't is so with a great many things.'

'I don't suppose likely you're goin' up to the Bowden reunion?' asked the hostess as the white horse lifted his head and we were saying good-bye.

'Why, yes,' said Mrs. Blackett and Mrs. Todd and I, all together.

'I am connected with the family. Yes, I expect to be there this afternoon. I've been lookin' forward to it,' she told us eagerly.

'We shall see you there. Come and sit with us if it's convenient,' said dear Mrs. Blackett, and we drove away.

'I wonder who she was before she was married?' said Mrs. Todd, who was usually unerring in matters of genealogy. 'She must have been one of that remote branch that lived down beyond Thomaston. We can find out this afternoon. I expect that the families'll march together, or be sorted out some way. I'm willing to own a relation that has such proper ideas of dough-nuts.'

'I seem to see the family looks,' said Mrs. Blackett. 'I wish we'd asked her name. She's a stranger, and I want to help make it pleasant for all such.'

'She resembles Cousin Pa'lina Bowden about the forehead,' said Mrs. Todd with decision.

We had just passed a piece of woodland that shaded the road, and come out to some open fields beyond, when Mrs. Todd suddenly reined in the horse as if somebody had stood on the roadside and stopped her. She even gave that quick reassuring nod of her head which was usually made to answer for a bow, but I discovered that she was looking eagerly at a tall ash-tree that grew just inside the field fence.

'I thought 't was goin' to do well,' she said complacently as we went on again. 'Last time I was up this way that tree was kind of drooping and discouraged. Grown trees act that way sometimes, same's folks; then they'll put right to it and strike their roots off into new ground and start all over again with real good courage. Ash-trees is very likely to have poor spells; they ain't got the resolution of other trees.'

I listened hopefully for more; it was this peculiar wisdom that made one value Mrs. Todd's pleasant company.

'There's sometimes a good hearty tree growin' right out of the bare rock, out o' some crack that just holds the roots;' she went on to say, 'right on the pitch o' one o' them bare stony hills where you can't seem to see a wheel-barrowful o' good earth in a place, but that tree keeps a green top in the driest summer. You lay your ear down to the ground an' you'll hear a little stream runnin'. Every such tree has got its own livin' spring; there's folks made to match 'em.'

I could not help turning to look at Mrs. Blackett, close beside me. Her hands were clasped placidly in their thin black woollen gloves, and she was looking at the flowery wayside as we went slowly along, with a pleased, expectant smile. I do not think she had heard a word about the trees.

'I just saw a nice plant o' elecampane growin' back there,' she said presently to her daughter.

'I haven't got my mind on herbs to-day,' responded Mrs. Todd, in the most matter-of-fact way. 'I'm bent on seeing folks,' and she shook the reins again.

I for one had no wish to hurry, it was so pleasant in the shady roads. The woods stood close to the road on the right; on the left were narrow fields and pastures where there were as many acres of spruces and pines as there were acres of bay and juniper and huckleberry, with a little turf between. When I thought we were in the heart of the inland country, we reached the top of a hill, and suddenly there lay spread out before us a wonderful great view of well-cleared fields that swept down to the wide water of a bay. Beyond this were distant shores like another country in the midday haze which half hid the hills beyond, and the far-away pale blue mountains on the northern horizon. There was a schooner with all sails set coming down the bay from a white village that was sprinkled on the shore, and there were many sailboats flitting about. It was a noble landscape, and my eyes, which had grown used to the narrow inspection of a shaded roadside, could hardly take it in.

'Why, it's the upper bay,' said Mrs. Todd. 'You can see 'way over into the town of Fessenden. Those farms 'way over there are all in Fessenden. Mother used to have a sister that lived up that shore. If we started as early's we could on a summer mornin', we couldn't get to her place from Green Island till late afternoon, even with a fair, steady breeze, and you had to strike the time just right so as to fetch up 'long o' the tide and land near the flood. 'T was ticklish business, an' we didn't visit back an' forth as much as mother desired. You have to go 'way down the co'st to Cold Spring Light an' round that long point – up here's what they call the Back Shore.'

'No, we were 'most always separated, my dear sister and me, after the first year she was married,' said Mrs. Blackett. 'We had our little families an' plenty o' cares. We were always lookin' forward to the time we could see each other more. Now and then she'd get out to the island for a few days while her husband'd go fishin'; and once he stopped with her an' two children, and made him some flakes right there and cured all his fish for winter. We did have a beautiful time together, sister an' me; she used to look back to it long's she lived.'

'I do love to look over there where she used to live,' Mrs. Blackett went on as we began to go down the hill. 'It seems as if she must still be there, though she's long been gone. She loved their farm, – she didn't see how I got so used to our island; but somehow I was always happy from the first.'

'Yes, it's very dull to me up among those slow farms,' declared Mrs. Todd. 'The snow troubles 'em in winter. They're all besieged by winter, as you may say; 't is far better by the shore than up among such places. I never thought I should like to live up country.'

'Why, just see the carriages ahead of us on the next rise!' exclaimed Mrs. Blackett. 'There's going to be a great gathering, don't you believe there is, Almiry? It hasn't seemed up to now as if anybody was going but us. An' 't is such a beautiful day, with yesterday cool and pleasant to work an' get ready, I shouldn't wonder if everybody was there, even the slow ones like Phebe Ann Brock.'

134

Mrs. Blackett's eyes were bright with excitement, and even Mrs. Todd showed remarkable enthusiasm. She hurried the horse and caught up with the holiday-makers ahead. 'There's all the Dep'fords goin', six in the waggon,' she told us joyfully; 'an' Mis' Alva Tilley's folks are now risin' the hill in their new carry-all.'

Mrs. Blackett pulled at the neat bow of her black bonnet-strings and tied them with careful precision. 'I believe your bonnet's on a little bit sideways, dear,' she advised Mrs. Todd as if she were a child; but Mrs. Todd was too much occupied to pay proper heed. We began to feel a new sense of gaiety and of taking part in the great occasion as we joined the little train.

CHAPTER EIGHTEEN

The Bowden Reunion

*

I⊤ is very rare in country life, where high days and holidays are few, that any occasion of general interest proves to be less than great. Such is the hidden fire of enthusiasm in the New England nature that, once given an outlet, it shines forth with almost volcanic light and heat. In quiet neighbourhoods such inward force does not waste itself upon those petty excitements of every day that belong to cities, but when, at long intervals, the altars to patriotism, to friendship, to the ties of kindred, are reared in our familiar fields, then the fires glow, the flames come up as if from the inexhaustible burning heart of the earth; the primal fires break through the granite dust in which our souls are set. Each heart is warm and every face shines with the ancient light. Such a day as this has transfiguring powers, and easily makes friends of those who have been cold-hearted, and gives to those who are dumb their chance to speak, and lends some beauty to the plainest face.

'Oh, I expect I shall meet friends to-day that I haven't seen in a long while,' said Mrs. Blackett with deep satisfaction. ''T will bring out a good many of the old folks, 't is such a lovely day. I'm always glad not to have them disappointed.'

'I guess likely the best of 'em 'll be there,' answered

Mrs. Todd with gentle humour, stealing a glance at me. 'There's one thing certain: there's nothing takes in this whole neighbourhood like anything related to the Bowdens. Yes, I do feel that when you call upon the Bowdens you may expect most families to rise up between the Landing and the far end of the Back Cove. Those that aren't kin by blood are kin by marriage.'

'There used to be an old story goin' about when I was a girl,' said Mrs. Blackett, with much amusement. 'There was a great many more Bowdens then than there are now, and the folks was all setting in meeting a dreadful hot Sunday afternoon, and a scatter-witted little bound girl came running to the meetin'-house door all out o' breath from somewheres in the neighbourhood. "Mis' Bowden, Mis' Bowden!" says she. "Your baby's in a fit!" They used to tell that the whole congregation was up on its feet in a minute and right out into the aisles. All the Mis' Bowdens was setting right out for home; the minister stood there in the pulpit tryin' to keep sober, an' all at once he burst right out laughin'. He was a very nice man, they said, and he said he'd better give 'em the benediction, and they could hear the sermon next Sunday, so he kept it over. My mother was there, and she thought certain 't was me.'

'None of our family was ever subject to fits,' interrupted Mrs. Todd severely. 'No, we never had fits, none of us, an 't was lucky we didn't 'way out there to Green Island. Now these folks right in front: dear sakes knows the bunches o' soothing catnip an' yarrow I've had to favour old Mis' Evins with dryin'! You can see it right in their expressions, all them Evins folks. There, just you look up to the cross-roads, mother,' she suddenly exclaimed. 'See all the teams ahead of us. And oh, look down on the bay; yes, look down on the bay! See what a sight o' boats, all headin' for the Bowden place cove!'

'Oh, ain't it beautiful!' said Mrs. Blackett, with all the delight of a girl. She stood up in the high waggon to see everything, and when she sat down again she took fast hold of my hand.

'Hadn't you better urge the horse a little, Almiry?' she asked. 'He's had it easy as we came along, and he can rest when we get there. The others are some little ways ahead, and I don't want to lose a minute.'

We watched the boats drop their sails one by one in the cove as we drove along the high land. The old Bowden house stood, low-storied and broad-roofed, in its green fields as if it were a motherly brown hen waiting for the flock that came straying toward it from every direction. The first Bowden settler had made his home there, and it was still the Bowden farm; five generations of sailors and farmers and soldiers had been its children. And presently Mrs. Blackett showed me the stone-walled burying-ground that stood like a little fort on a knoll overlooking the bay, but, as she said, there were plenty of scattered Bowdens who were not laid there,— some lost at sea and some out West, and some who died in the war; most of the home graves were those of women.

We could see now that there were different footpaths from along shore and across country. In all these there were straggling processions walking in single file, like old illustrations of the Pilgrim's Progress. There was a crowd about the house as if huge bees were swarming in the lilac bushes. Beyond the fields and cove a higher point of land ran out into the bay, covered with woods which must have kept away much of the northwest wind in winter. Now there was a pleasant look of shade and shelter there for the great family meeting.

We hurried on our way, beginning to feel as if we were very late, and it was a great satisfaction at last to turn out of the stony highroad into a green lane shaded with old apple-trees. Mrs. Todd encouraged the horse until he fairly pranced with gaiety as we drove round to the front of the house on the soft turf. There was an instant cry of rejoicing, and two or three persons ran toward us from the busy group.

'Why, dear Mis' Blackett! – here's Mis' Blackett!' I heard them say, as if it were pleasure enough for one day to have a sight of her. Mrs. Todd turned to me with a lovely look of triumph and self-forgetfulness. An elderly man who wore the look of a prosperous sea-captain put up both arms and lifted Mrs. Blackett down from the high waggon like a child, and kissed her with hearty affection. 'I was master afraid she wouldn't

be here,' he said, looking at Mrs. Todd with a face like
a happy sunburnt schoolboy, while everybody crowded
round to give their welcome.

'Mother's always the queen,' said Mrs. Todd. 'Yes,
they'll all make everything of mother; she'll have a
lovely time to-day. I wouldn't have had her miss it,
and there won't be a thing she'll ever regret, except to
mourn because William wa'n't here.'

Mrs. Blackett having been properly escorted to the
house, Mrs. Todd received her own full share of
honour, and some of the men with a simple kindness
that was the soul of chivalry, waited upon us and our
baskets and led away the white horse. I already knew
some of Mrs. Todd's friends and kindred, and felt like
an adopted Bowden in this happy moment. It seemed
to be enough for any one to have arrived by the same
conveyance as Mrs. Blackett, who presently had her
court inside the house, while Mrs. Todd, large, hospitable, and preeminent, was the centre of a rapidly
increasing crowd about the lilac bushes. Small companies were continually coming up the long green
slope from the water, and nearly all the boats had come
to shore. I counted three or four that were baffled by
the light breeze, but before long all the Bowdens,
small and great, seemed to have assembled, and we
started to go up to the grove across the field.

Out of the chattering crowd of noisy children, and
large-waisted women whose best black dresses fell
straight to the ground in generous folds, and sunburnt

men who looked as serious as if it were town-meeting
day, there suddenly came silence and order. I saw the
straight, soldierly little figure of a man who bore a
fine resemblance to Mrs. Blackett, and who appeared
to marshal us with perfect ease. He was imperative
enough, but with a grand military sort of courtesy,
and bore himself with solemn dignity of importance.
We were sorted out according to some clear design of
his own, and stood as speechless as a troop to await his
orders. Even the children were ready to march together,
a pretty flock, and at the last moment Mrs. Blackett and
a few distinguished companions, the ministers and
those who were very old, came out of the house together
and took their places. We ranked by fours, and even
then we made a long procession.

There was a wide path mowed for us across the
field, and, as we moved along, the birds flew up out
of the thick second crop of clover, and the bees hummed
as if it still were June. There was a flashing of white
gulls over the water where the fleet of boats rode the
low waves together in the cove, swaying their small
masts as if they kept time to our steps. The plash of
the water could be heard faintly, yet still be heard;
we might have been a company of ancient Greeks
going to celebrate a victory, or to worship the god of
harvests in the grove above. It was strangely moving
to see this and to make part of it. The sky, the sea,
have watched poor humanity at its rites so long; we
were no more a New England family celebrating its

own existence and simple progress; we carried the tokens and inheritance of all such households from which this had descended, and were only the latest of our line. We possessed the instincts of a far, forgotten childhood; I found myself thinking that we ought to be carrying green branches and singing as we went. So we came to the thick shaded grove still silent, and were set in our places by the straight trees that swayed together and let sunshine through here and there like a single golden leaf that flickered down, vanishing in the cool shade.

The grove was so large that the great family looked far smaller than it had in the open field; there was a thick growth of dark pines and firs with an occasional maple or oak that gave a gleam of colour like a bright window in the great roof. On three sides we could see the water, shining behind the tree-trunks, and feel the cool salt breeze that began to come up with the tide just as the day reached its highest point of heat. We could see the green sunlit field we had just crossed as if we looked out at it from a dark room, and the old house and its lilacs standing placidly in the sun, and the great barn with stockade of carriages from which two or three care-taking men who had lingered were coming across the field together. Mrs. Todd had taken off her warm gloves and looked the picture of content.

'There!' she exclaimed. 'I've always meant to have you see this place, but I never looked for such a beautiful opportunity – weather an' occasion both made to match. Yes, it suits me: I don't ask no more. I want to know if you saw mother walkin' at the head! It choked me right up to see mother at the head, walkin' with the ministers,' and Mrs. Todd turned away to hide the feelings she could not instantly control.

'Who was the marshal?' I hastened to ask. 'Was he an old soldier?'

'Don't he do well?' answered Mrs. Todd with satisfaction.

'He don't often have such a chance to show off his gifts,' said Mrs. Caplin, a friend from the Landing who had joined us. 'That's Sant Bowden; he always takes the lead, such days. Good for nothing else most o' his time; trouble is, he' –

I turned with interest to hear the worst. Mrs. Caplin's tone was both zealous and impressive.

'Stim'lates,' she explained scornfully.

'No, Santin' never was in the war,' said Mrs. Todd with lofty indifference. 'It was a cause of real distress to him. He kep' enlistin', and travelled far an' wide about here, an' even took the bo't and went to Boston to volunteer; but he ain't a sound man, an' they wouldn't have him. They say he knows all their tactics, an' can tell all about the battle o' Waterloo well's he can Bunker Hill. I told him once the country 'd lost a great general, an' I meant it, too.'

'I expect you're near right,' said Mrs. Caplin, a little crestfallen and apologetic.

'I be right,' insisted Mrs. Todd with much amiability. "T was most too bad to cramp him down to his peaceful trade, but he's a most excellent shoemaker at his best, an' he always says it's a trade that gives him time to think an' plan his manœuvres. Over to the Port they always invite him to march Decoration Day, same as the rest, an' he does look noble; he comes of soldier stock.'

I had been noticing with great interest the curiously French type of face which prevailed in this rustic company. I had said to myself before that Mrs. Blackett was plainly of French descent, in both her appearance and her charming gifts, but this is not surprising when one has learned how large a proportion of the early settlers on this northern coast of New England were of Huguenot blood, and that it is the Norman Englishman, not the Saxon, who goes adventuring to a new world.

'They used to say in old times,' said Mrs. Todd modestly, 'that our family came of very high folks in France, and one of 'em was a great general in some o' the old wars. I sometimes think that Santin's ability has come 'way down from then. 'T ain't nothin' he's ever acquired; 't was born in him. I don't know's he ever saw a fine parade, or met with those that studied up such things. He's figured it all out an' got his papers so he knows how to aim a cannon right for William's fish-house five miles out on Green Island, or up there on Burnt Island where the signal is. He had it all over to me one day, an' I tried hard to appear interested. His life's all in it, but he will have those poor gloomy spells come over him now an' then, an' then he has to drink.'

Mrs. Caplin gave a heavy sigh.

'There's a great many such strayaway folks, just as there is plants,' continued Mrs. Todd, who was nothing if not botanical. 'I know of just one sprig of laurel that grows over back here in a wild spot, an' I never could hear of no other on this coast. I had a large bunch brought me once from Massachusetts way, so I know it. This piece grows in an open spot where you'd think 't would do well, but it's sort o' poor-lookin'. I've visited it time an' again, just to notice its poor blooms. 'T is a real Sant Bowden, out of its own place.'

Mrs. Caplin looked bewildered and blank. 'Well, all I know is, last year he worked out some kind of a plan so's to parade the county conference in platoons, and got 'em all flustered up tryin' to sense his ideas of a holler square,' she burst forth, 'They was holler enough anyway after ridin' 'way down from up country into the salt air, and they'd been treated to a sermon on faith an' works from old Fayther Harlow that never knows when to cease. 'T wa'n't no time for tactics then, – they wa'n't a-thinkin' of the church military. Sant, he couldn't do nothin' with 'em. All he thinks of, when he sees a crowd, is how to march 'em. 'T is all very well when he don't 'tempt too much. He never did act like other folks.'

'Ain't I just been maintainin' that he ain't like

'em?' urged Mrs. Todd decidedly. 'Strange folks has got to have strange ways, for what I see.'

'Somebody observed once that you could pick out the likeness of 'most every sort of a foreigner when you looked about you in our parish,' said Sister Caplin, her face brightening with sudden illumination. 'I didn't see the bearin' of it then quite so plain. I always did think Mari' Harris resembled a Chinee.'

'Mari' Harris was pretty as a child, I remember,' said the pleasant voice of Mrs. Blackett, who, after receiving the affectionate greetings of nearly the whole company, came to join us,— to see, as she insisted, that we were out of mischief.

'Yes, Mari' was one o' them pretty little lambs that make dreadful homely old sheep,' replied Mrs. Todd with energy. 'Cap'n Littlepage never'd look so disconsolate if she was any sort of a proper person to direct things. She might divert him; yes, she might divert the old gentleman, an' let him think he had his own way, 'stead o' arguing everything down to the bare bone. 'T wouldn't hurt her to sit down an' hear his great stories once in a while.'

'The stories are very interesting,' I ventured to say.

'Yes, you always catch yourself a-thinkin' what if they was all true, and he had the right of it,' answered Mrs. Todd. 'He's a good sight better company, though dreamy, than such sordid creatur's as Mari' Harris.'

'Live and let live,' said dear old Mrs. Blackett gently. 'I haven't seen the captain for a good while, now that

I ain't so constant to meetin',' she added wistfully. 'We always have known each other.'

'Why, if it is a good pleasant day to-morrow, I'll get William to call an' invite the capt'in to dinner. William'll be in early so's to pass up the street without meetin' anybody.'

'There, they're callin' out it's time to set the tables,' said Mrs. Caplin, with great excitement.

'Here's Cousin Sarah Jane Blackett! Well, I am pleased, certain!' exclaimed Mrs. Todd, with unaffected delight; and these kindred spirits met and parted with the promise of a good talk later on. After this there was no more time for conversation until we were seated in order at the long tables.

'I'm one that always dreads seeing some o' the folks that I don't like, at such a time as this,' announced Mrs. Todd privately to me after a season of reflection. We were just waiting for the feast to begin. 'You wouldn't think such a great creatur' 's I be could feel all over pins an' needles. I remember, the day I promised to Nathan, how it come over me, just's I was feelin' happy's I could, that I'd got to have an own cousin o' his for my near relation all the rest o' my life, an' it seemed as if die I should. Poor Nathan saw somethin' had crossed me,—he had very nice feelings,—and when he asked me what 't was, I told him. "I never could like her myself," said he. "You sha'n't be bothered, dear," he says; an' 't was one o' the things that made me set a good deal by Nathan, he didn't make a habit of always opposin', like some men. "Yes," says I, "but think o' Thanksgivin' times an' funerals; she's our relation, an' we've got to own her." Young folks don't think o' those things. There she goes now, do let's pray her by!' said Mrs. Todd, with an alarming transition from general opinions to particular animosities. 'I hate her just the same as I always did; but she's got on a real pretty dress. I do try to remember that she's Nathan's cousin. Oh dear, well; she's gone by after all, an' ain't seen me. I expected she'd come pleasantin' round just to show off an' say afterwards she was acquainted.'

This was so different from Mrs. Todd's usual largeness of mind that I had a moment's uneasiness; but the cloud passed quickly over her spirit, and was gone with the offender.

There never was a more generous out-of-door feast along the coast than the Bowden family set forth that day. To call it a picnic would make it seem trivial. The great tables were edged with pretty oak-leaf trimming, which the boys and girls made. We brought flowers from the fence-thickets of the great field; and out of the disorder of flowers and provisions suddenly appeared as orderly a scheme for the feast as the marshal had shaped for the procession. I began to respect the Bowdens for their inheritance of good taste and skill and a certain pleasing gift of formality. Something made them do all these things in a finer way than most

country people would have done them. As I looked up
and down the tables there was a good cheer, a grave
soberness that shone with pleasure, a humble dignity of
bearing. There were some who should have sat below
the salt for lack of this good breeding; but they were
not many. So, I said to myself, their ancestors may have
sat in the great hall of some old French house in the
Middle Ages, when battles and sieges and processions
and feasts were familiar things. The ministers and
Mrs. Blackett, with a few of their rank and age, were
put in places of honour, and for once that I looked any
other way I looked twice at Mrs. Blackett's face,
serene and mindful of privilege and responsibility, the
mistress by simple fitness of this great day.

Mrs. Todd looked up at the roof of green trees,
and then carefully surveyed the company. 'I see 'em
better now they're all settin' down,' she said with
satisfaction. 'There's old Mr. Gilbraith and his sister.
I wish they were settin' with us; they're not among
folks they can parley with, an' they look disappointed.'

As the feast went on, the spirits of my companion
steadily rose. The excitement of an unexpectedly great
occasion was a subtle stimulant to her disposition, and I
could see that sometimes when Mrs. Todd had seemed
limited and heavily domestic, she had simply grown
sluggish for lack of proper surroundings. She was not
so much reminiscent now as expectant, and as alert
and gay as a girl. We who were her neighbours were
full of gaiety, which was but the reflected light from

her beaming countenance. It was not the first time that I was full of wonder at the waste of human ability in this world, as a botanist wonders at the wastefulness of nature, the thousand seeds that die, the unused provision of every sort. The reserve force of society grows more and more amazing to one's thought. More than one face among the Bowdens showed that only opportunity and stimulus were lacking,— a narrow set of circumstances had caged a fine able character and held it captive. One sees exactly the same types in a country gathering as in the most brilliant city company. You are safe to be understood if the spirit of your speech is the same for one neighbour as for the other.

CHAPTER NINETEEN

The Feast's End

*

THE feast was a noble feast, as has already been said. There was an elegant ingenuity displayed in the form of pies which delighted my heart. Once acknowledge that an American pie is far to be preferred to its humble ancestor, the English tart, and it is joyful to be reassured at a Bowden reunion that invention has not yet failed. Beside a delightful variety of material, the decorations went beyond all my former experience; dates and names were wrought in lines of pastry and frosting on the tops. There was even more elaborate reading matter on an excellent early-apple pie which we began to share and eat, precept upon precept. Mrs. Todd helped me generously to the whole word *Bowden*, and consumed *Reunion* herself, save an undecipherable fragment; but the most renowned essay in cookery on the tables was a model of the old Bowden house made of durable gingerbread, with all the windows and doors in the right places, and sprigs of genuine lilac set at the front. It must have been baked in sections, in one of the last of the great brick ovens, and fastened together on the morning of the day. There was a general sigh when this fell into ruin at the feast's end, and it was shared by a great part of the assembly, not without seriousness, and as if it were a pledge and token of loyalty. I met the maker of the gingerbread house, which had called up lively remembrances of a childish story. She had the gleaming eye of an enthusiast and a look of high ideals.

'I could just as well have made it all of frosted cake,' she said, 'but 't wouldn't have been the right shade; the old house, as you observe, was never painted, and I concluded that plain gingerbread would represent it best. It wasn't all I expected it would be,' she said sadly, as many an artist had said before her of his work.

There were speeches by the ministers; and there proved to be a historian among the Bowdens, who gave some fine anecdotes of the family history; and then appeared a poetess, whom Mrs. Todd regarded with wistful compassion and indulgence, and when the long faded garland of verses came to an appealing end, she turned to me with words of praise.

'Sounded pretty,' said the generous listener. 'Yes, I thought she did very well. We went to school together, an' Mary Anna had a very hard time; trouble was, her mother thought she'd given birth to a genius, an' Mary Anna's come to believe it herself. There, I don't know what we should have done without her; there ain't nobody else that can write poetry between here and 'way up toward Rockland; it adds a great deal at such a time. When she speaks o' those that are gone, she feels it all, and so does everybody else, but she harps too much. I'd laid half of that away for next time, if I was Mary Anna. There comes mother to speak to her, an' old Mr. Gilbraith's sister; now she'll be heartened right up. Mother'll say just the right thing.'

The leave-takings were as affecting as the meetings of these old friends had been. There were enough young persons at the reunion, but it is the old who really value such opportunities; as for the young, it is the habit of every day to meet their comrades, – the time of separation has not come. To see the joy with which these elder kinsfolk and acquaintances had looked in one another's faces, and the lingering touch of their friendly hands; to see these affectionate meetings and then the reluctant partings, gave one a new idea of the isolation in which it was possible to live in that after all thinly settled region. They did not expect to see one another again very soon; the steady, hard work on the farms, the difficulty of getting from place to place, especially in winter when boats were laid up, gave double value to any occasion which could bring a large number of families together. Even funerals in this country of the pointed firs were not without their social advantages and satisfactions. I heard the words 'next summer' repeated many times, though summer was still ours and all the leaves were green.

The boats began to put out from shore, and the waggons to drive away. Mrs. Blackett took me into the old house when we came back from the grove: it was her father's birthplace and early home, and she had spent much of her own childhood there with her grandmother. She spoke of those days as if they had but lately passed; in fact, I could imagine that the house looked almost exactly the same to her. I could see the brown rafters of the unfinished roof as I looked up the steep staircase, though the best room was as handsome with its good wainscoting and touch of ornament on the cornice as any old room of its day in a town.

Some of the guests who came from a distance were still sitting in the best room when we went in to take leave of the master and mistress of the house. We all said eagerly what a pleasant day it had been, and how swiftly the time had passed. Perhaps it is the great national anniversaries which our country has lately kept, and the soldiers' meetings that take place everywhere, which have made reunions of every sort the fashion. This one, at least, had been very interesting. I fancied that old feuds had been overlooked, and the old saying that blood is thicker than water had again proved itself true, though from the variety of names one argued a certain adulteration of the Bowden traits and belongings. Clannishness is an instinct of the heart,— it is more than a birthright, or a custom; and lesser rights were forgotten in the claim to a common inheritance.

We were among the very last to return to our proper lives and lodgings. I came near to feeling like a true Bowden, and parted from certain new friends as if they were old friends; we were rich with the treasure of a new remembrance.

At last we were in the high waggon again; the old white horse had been well fed in the Bowden barn, and we drove away and soon began to climb the long hill toward the wooded ridge. The road was new to me, as roads always are, going back. Most of our companions had been full of anxious thoughts of home,— of the cows, or of young children likely to fall into disaster,— but we had no reason for haste, and drove slowly along, talking and resting by the way. Mrs. Todd said once that she really hoped her front door had been shut on account of the dust blowing in, but added that nothing made any weight on her mind except not to forget to turn a few late mullein leaves that were drying on a newspaper in the little loft. Mrs. Blackett and I gave our word of honour that we would remind her of this heavy responsibility. The way seemed short, we had so much to talk about. We climbed hills where we could see the great bay and the islands, and then went down into shady valleys where the air began to feel like evening, cool and damp with a fragrance of wet ferns. Mrs. Todd alighted once or twice, refusing all assistance in securing some boughs of a rare shrub which she valued for its bark, though she proved incommunicative as to her reasons. We passed the house where we had been so kindly entertained with doughnuts earlier in the day, and found it closed and deserted, which was a disappointment.

'They must have stopped to tea somewheres and thought they'd finish up the day,' said Mrs. Todd.

'Those that enjoyed it best'll want to get right home so's to think it over.'

'I didn't see the woman there after all, did you?' asked Mrs. Blackett as the horse stopped to drink at the trough.

'Oh yes, I spoke with her,' answered Mrs. Todd, with but scant interest or approval. 'She ain't a member o' our family.'

'I thought you said she resembled Cousin Pa'lina Bowden about the forehead,' suggested Mrs. Blackett.

'Well, she don't,' answered Mrs. Todd impatiently. 'I ain't one that's ord'narily mistaken about family likenesses, and she didn't seem to meet with friends, so I went square up to her. "I expect you're a Bowden by your looks," says I. "Yes, I take it you're one o' the Bowdens." "Lor', no", says she. "Dennett was my maiden name, but I married a Bowden for my first husband. I thought I'd come an' just see what was a-goin' on!"'

Mrs. Blackett laughed heartily. 'I'm goin' to remember to tell William o' that,' she said. 'There, Almiry, the only thing that's troubled me all this day is to think how William would have enjoyed it. I do so wish William had been there.'

'I sort of wish he had, myself,' said Mrs. Todd frankly.

'There wa'n't many old folks there, somehow,' said Mrs. Blackett, with a touch of sadness in her voice. 'There ain't so many to come as there used to be, I'm aware, but I expected to see more.'

'I thought they turned out pretty well, when you come to think of it; why, everybody was sayin' so an' feelin' gratified,' answered Mrs. Todd hastily with pleasing unconsciousness; then I saw the quick colour flash into her cheek, and presently she made some excuse to turn and steal an anxious look at her mother. Mrs. Blackett was smiling and thinking about her happy day, though she began to look a little tired. Neither of my companions was troubled by her burden of years. I hoped in my heart that I might be like them as I lived on into age, and then smiled to think that I too was no longer very young. So we always keep the same hearts, though our outer framework fails and shows the touch of time.

' 'T was pretty when they sang the hymn, wasn't it?' asked Mrs. Blackett at supper-time, with real enthusiasm. 'There was such a plenty o' men's voices; where I sat it did sound beautiful. I had to stop and listen when they came to the last verse.'

I saw that Mrs. Todd's broad shoulders began to shake. 'There was good singers there; yes, there was excellent singers,' she agreed heartily, putting down her teacup, 'but I chanced to drift alongside Mis' Peter Bowden o' Great Bay, an' I couldn't help thinkin' if she was as far out o' town as she was out o' tune, she wouldn't get back in a day.'

CHAPTER TWENTY

Along Shore

✳

ONE day as I went along the shore beyond the old wharves and the newer, high-stepped fabric of the steamer landing, I saw that all the boats were beached, and the slack water period of the early afternoon prevailed. Nothing was going on, not even the most leisurely of occupations, like baiting trawls or mending nets, or repairing lobster pots; the very boats seemed to be taking an afternoon nap in the sun. I could hardly discover a distant sail as I looked seaward, except a weather-beaten lobster smack, which seemed to have been taken for a plaything by the light airs that blew about the bay. She drifted and turned about so aimlessly in the wide reach off Burnt Island, that I suspected there was nobody at the wheel, or that she might have parted her rusty anchor chain while all the crew were asleep.

I watched her for a minute or two; she was the old *Miranda*, owned by some of the Caplins, and I knew her by an odd shaped patch of newish duck that was set into the peak of her dingy mainsail. Her vagaries offered such an exciting subject for conversation that my heart rejoiced at the sound of a hoarse voice behind me. At that moment, before I had time to answer, I saw something large and shapeless flung from the *Miranda's* deck that splashed the water high against

158

her black side, and my companion gave a satisfied chuckle. The old lobster smack's sail caught the breeze again at this moment, and she moved off down the bay. Turning, I found old Elijah Tilley, who had come softly out of his dark fish-house, as if it were a burrow.

'Boy got kind o' drowsy steerin' of her; Monroe he hove him right overboard; 'wake now fast enough,' explained Mr. Tilley, and we laughed together.

I was delighted, for my part, that the vicissitudes and dangers of the *Miranda*, in a rocky channel, should have given me this opportunity to make acquaintance with an old fisherman to whom I had never spoken. At first he had seemed to be one of those evasive and uncomfortable persons who are so suspicious of you that they make you almost suspicious of yourself. Mr. Elijah Tilley appeared to regard a stranger with scornful indifference. You might see him standing on the pebble beach or in a fish-house doorway, but when you came nearer he was gone. He was one of the small company of elderly, gaunt-shaped great fishermen whom I used to like to see leading up a deep-laden boat by the head, as if it were a horse, from the water's edge to the steep slope of the pebble beach. There were four of these large old men at the Landing, who were the survivors of an earlier and more vigorous generation. There was an alliance and understanding between them, so close that it was apparently speechless. They gave much time to watching one another's boats go out or come in; they lent a ready hand at tending one another's lobster traps in rough weather; they helped to clean the fish, or to sliver porgies for the trawls, as if they were in close partnership; and when a boat came in from deep-sea fishing they were never far out of the way, and hastened to help carry it ashore, two by two, splashing alongside, or holding its steady head, as if it were a wilful sea colt. As a matter of fact no boat could help being steady and way-wise under their instant direction and companionship. Abel's boat and Jonathan Bowden's boat were as distinct and experienced personalities as the men themselves, and as inexpressive. Arguments and opinions were unknown to the conversation of these ancient friends; you would as soon have expected to hear small talk in a company of elephants as to hear old Mr. Bowden or Elijah Tilley and their two mates waste breath upon any form of trivial gossip. They made brief statements to one another from time to time. As you came to know them you wondered more and more that they should talk at all. Speech seemed to be a light and elegant accomplishment, and their unexpected acquaintance with its arts made them of new value to the listener. You felt almost as if a landmark pine should suddenly address you in regard to the weather, or a lofty-minded old camel make a remark as you stood respectfully near him under the circus tent.

I often wondered a great deal about the inner life and thought of these self-contained old fishermen;

their minds seemed to be fixed upon nature and the elements rather than upon any contrivances of man, like politics or theology. My friend, Captain Bowden, who was the nephew of the eldest of this group, regarded them with deference; but he did not belong to their secret companionship, though he was neither young nor talkative.

'They've gone together ever since they were boys, they know most everything about the sea amon'st them,' he told me once. 'They was always just as you see 'em now since the memory of man.'

These ancient seafarers had houses and lands not outwardly different from other Dunnet Landing dwellings, and two of them were fathers of families, but their true dwelling places were the sea, and the stony beach that edged its familiar shore, and the fish-houses, where much salt brine from the mackerel kits had soaked the very timbers into a state of brown permanence and petrifaction. It had also affected the old fishermen's hard complexions, until one fancied that when Death claimed them it could only be with the aid, not of any slender modern dart, but the good serviceable harpoon of a seventeenth century woodcut.

Elijah Tilley was such an evasive, discouraged-looking person, heavy-headed, and stooping so that one could never look him in the face, that even after his friendly exclamation about Monroe Pennell, the lobster smack's skipper, and the sleepy boy, I did not venture at once to speak again. Mr. Tilley was carrying a small haddock in one hand, and presently shifted it to the other hand lest it might touch my skirt. I knew that my company was accepted, and we walked together a little way.

'You mean to have a good supper,' I ventured to say, by way of friendliness.

'Goin' to have this 'ere haddock an' some o' my good baked potatoes; must eat to live,' responded my companion with great pleasantness and open approval. I found that I had suddenly left the forbidding coast and come into a smooth little harbour of friendship.

'You ain't never been up to my place,' said the old man. 'Folks don't come now as they used to; no, 't ain't no use to ask folks now. My poor dear she was a great hand to draw young company.'

I remembered that Mrs. Todd had once said that this old fisherman had been sore stricken and unconsoled at the death of his wife.

'I should like very much to come,' said I. 'Perhaps you are going to be at home later on?'

Mr. Tilley agreed, by a sober nod, and went his way bent-shouldered and with a rolling gait. There was a new patch high on the shoulder of his old waistcoat, which corresponded to the renewing of the *Miranda's* mainsail down the bay, and I wondered if his own fingers, clumsy with much deep-sea fishing, had set it in.

'Was there a good catch to-day?' I asked, stopping a

moment. 'I didn't happen to be on the shore when the boats came in.'

'No; all come in pretty light,' answered Mr. Tilley. 'Addicks an' Bowden they done the best; Abel an' me we had but a slim fare. We went out 'arly, but not so 'arly as sometimes; looked like a poor mornin'. I got nine haddick, all small, and seven fish; the rest on 'em got more fish than haddick. Well, I don't expect they feel like bitin' every day; we l'arn to humour 'em a little, an' let 'em have their way 'bout it. These plaguey dog-fish kind of worry 'em.' Mr. Tilley pronounced the last sentence with much sympathy, as if he looked upon himself as a true friend of all the haddock and codfish that lived on the fishing grounds, and so we parted.

Later in the afternoon I went along the beach again until I came to the foot of Mr. Tilley's land, and found his rough track across the cobble-stones and rocks to the field edge, where there was a heavy piece of old wreck timber, like a ship's bone, full of tree-nails. From this a little footpath, narrow with one man's treading, led up across the small green field that made Mr. Tilley's whole estate, except a straggling pasture that tilted on edge up the steep hillside beyond the house and road. I could hear the tinkle-tankle of a cow-bell somewhere among the spruces by which the pasture was being walked over and forested from every side; it was likely to be called the wood lot before long, but the field was unmolested. I could not see a bush or a brier anywhere within its walls, and hardly a stray pebble showed itself. This was most surprising in that country of firm ledges, and scattered stones which all the walls that industry could devise had hardly begun to clear away off the land. In the narrow field I noticed some stout stakes, apparently planted at random in the grass and among the hills of potatoes, but carefully painted yellow and white to match the house, a neat sharp-edged little dwelling, which looked strangely modern for its owner. I should have much sooner believed that the smart young wholesale egg merchant of the Landing was its occupant than Mr. Tilley, since a man's house is really but his larger body, and expresses in a way his nature and character.

I went up the field, following the smooth little path to the side door. As for using the front door, that was a matter of great ceremony; the long grass grew close against the high stone step, and a snowberry bush leaned over it, top-heavy with the weight of a morning-glory vine that had managed to take what the fishermen might call a half hitch about the door-knob. Elijah Tilley came to the side door to receive me; he was knitting a blue yarn stocking without looking on, and was warmly dressed for the season in a thick blue flannel shirt with white crockery buttons, a faded waistcoat and trousers heavily patched at the knees. These were not his fishing clothes. There was some-thing delightful in the grasp of his hand, warm and clean, as if it never touched anything but the comfortable woollen yarn, instead of cold sea water and slippery fish.

'What are the painted stakes for, down in the field?' I hastened to ask, and he came out a step or two along the path to see; and looked at the stakes as if his attention were called to them for the first time.

'Folks laughed at me when I first bought this place an' come here to live,' he explained. 'They said 't w'an't no kind of a field privilege at all; no place to raise anything, all full o' stones. I was aware it was good land, an' I worked some on it – odd times when I didn't have nothin' else on hand – till I cleared them loose stones all out. You never see a prettier piece than 't is now; now did ye? Well, as for them painted marks, them's my buoys. I struck on to some heavy rocks that didn't show none, but a plough'd be liable to ground on 'em, an' so I ketched holt an' buoyed 'em same's you see. They don't trouble me no more'n if they wa'n't there.'

'You haven't been to sea for nothing,' I said laughing.

'One trade helps another,' said Elijah with an amiable smile. 'Come right in an' set down. Come in an' rest ye,' he exclaimed, and led the way into his comfortable kitchen. The sunshine poured in at the two further windows, and a cat was curled up sound asleep on the table that stood between them. There was a new-looking light oilcloth of a tiled pattern on the floor, and a crockery teapot, large for a household of

only one person, stood on the bright stove. I ventured
to say that somebody must be a very good housekeeper.

'That's me,' acknowledged the old fisherman with
frankness. 'There ain't nobody here but me. I try
to keep things looking right, same's poor dear left 'em.
You set down here in this chair, then you can look off
an' see the water. None on 'em thought I was goin'
to get along alone, no way, but I wa'n' goin' to have
my house turned upsi' down an' all changed about; no,
not to please nobody. I was the only one knew just
how she liked to have things set, poor dear, an' I said
I was goin' to make shift, and I have made shift. I'd
rather tough it out alone.' And he sighed heavily, as if
to sigh were his familiar consolation.

We were both silent for a minute; the old man
looked out of the window, as if he had forgotten I was
there.

'You must miss her very much?' I said at last.

'I do miss her,' he answered, and sighed again. 'Folks
all kep' repeatin' that time would ease me, but I can't
find it does. No, I miss her just the same every day.'

'How long is it since she died?' I asked.

'Eight year now, come the first of October. It don't
seem near so long. I've got a sister that comes and
stops 'long o' me a little spell, spring an' fall, an' odd
times if I send after her. I ain't near so good a hand to
sew as I be to knit, and she's very quick to set everything to rights. She's a married woman with a family;
her son's folks lives at home, an' I can't make no great

claim on her time. But it makes me a kind o' good excuse, when I do send, to help her a little; she ain't none too well off. Poor dear always liked her, and we used to contrive our ways together. 'T is full as easy to be alone. I set here an' think it all over, an' think considerable when the weather's bad to go outside. I get so some days it feels as if poor dear might step right back into this kitchen. I keep a watchin' them doors as if she might step in to ary one. Yes, ma'am, I keep a-lookin' off an' droppin' o' my stitches; that's just how it seems. I can't git over losin' of her no way nor no how. Yes, ma'am, that's just how it seems to me.'

I did not say anything, and he did not look up.

'I git feelin' so sometimes I have to lay everything by an' go out door. She was a sweet pretty creatur' long's she lived,' the old man added mournfully. 'There's that little rockin' chair o' her'n, I set an' notice it an' think how strange 't is a creatur' like her should be gone an' that chair be here right in its old place.'

'I wish I had known her; Mrs. Todd told me about your wife one day,' I said.

'You'd have liked to come and see her; all the folks did,' said poor Elijah. 'She'd been so pleased to hear everything and see somebody new that took such an int'rest. She had a kind o' gift to make it pleasant for folks. I guess likely Almiry Todd told you she was a pretty woman, especially in her young days; late years, too, she kep' her looks and come to be so pleasant lookin'. There, 't ain't so much matter, I shall be done afore a great while. No; I shan't trouble the fish a great sight more.'

The old widower sat with his head bowed over his knitting, as if he were hastily shortening the very thread of time. The minutes went slowly by. He stopped his work and clasped his hands firmly together. I saw he had forgotten his guest, and I kept the afternoon watch with him. At last he looked up as if but a moment had passed of his continual loneliness.

'Yes, ma'am, I'm one that has seen trouble,' he said. and began to knit again.

The visible tribute of his careful house-keeping, and the clean bright room which had once enshrined his wife, and now enshrined her memory, was very moving to me; he had no thought for any one else or for any other place. I began to see her myself in her home,— a delicate-looking, faded little woman, who leaned upon his rough strength and affectionate heart, who was always watching for his boat out of this very window, and who always opened the door and welcomed him when he came home.

'I used to laugh at her, poor dear,' said Elijah, as if he read my thought. 'I used to make light of her timid notions. She used to be fearful when I was out in bad weather or baffled about gittin' ashore. She used to say the time seemed long to her, but I've found out all about it now. I used to be dreadful thoughtless when I was a young man and the fish was bitin' well. I'd stay out late some o' them days, an' I expect she'd watch an' watch an' lose heart a-waitin'. My heart alive! what a supper she'd git, an' be right there watchin' from the door, with somethin' over her head if 't was cold, waitin' to hear all about it as I come up the field. Lord, how I think o' all them little things!

'This was what she called the best room; in this way,' he said presently, laying his knitting on the table, and leading the way across the front entry and unlocking a door, which he threw open with an air of pride. The best room seemed to me a much sadder and more empty place than the kitchen; its conventionalities lacked the simple perfection of the humbler room and failed on the side of poor ambition; it was only when one remembered what patient saving, and what high respect for society in the abstract go to such furnishing that the little parlour was interesting at all. I could imagine the great day of certain purchases, the be-wildering shops of the next large town, the aspiring anxious woman, the clumsy sea-tanned man in his best clothes, so eager to be pleased, but at ease only when they were safe back in the sail-boat again, going down the bay with their precious freight, the hoarded money all spent and nothing to think of but tiller and sail. I looked at the unworn carpet, the glass vases on the mantelpiece with their prim bunches of bleached swamp grass and dusty marsh rosemary, and I could read the history of Mrs. Tilley's best room from its very beginning.

'You see for yourself what beautiful rugs she could

make; now I'm going to show you her best tea things she thought so much of,' said the master of the house, opening the door of a shallow cupboard. 'That's real chiny, all of it on those two shelves,' he told me proudly. 'I bought it all myself, when we was first married, in the port of Bordeaux. There never was one single piece of it broke until – Well, I used to say, long as she lived, there never was a piece broke, but long at the last I noticed she'd look kind o' distressed, an' I thought 't was 'count o' me boastin'. When they asked if they should use it when the folks was here to supper, time o' her funeral, I knew she'd want to have everything nice, and I said "certain." Some o' the women they come runnin' to me an' called me, while they was talkin' of the chiny down, an' showed me there was one o' the cups broke an' the pieces wropped in paper and pushed way back here, corner o' the shelf. They didn't want me to go an' think they done it. Poor dear! I had to put right out o' the house when I see that. I knowed in one minute how 't was. We'd got so used to sayin' 't was all there just's I fetched it home, an' so when she broke that cup somehow or 'nother she couldn't frame no words to come an' tell me. She couldn't think 't would vex me, 't was her own hurt pride. I guess there wa'n't no other secret ever lay between us.'

The French cups with their gay sprigs of pink and blue, the best tumblers, an old flowered bowl and tea caddy, and a japanned waiter or two adorned the shelves. These, with a few daguerreotypes in a little square pile, had the closet to themselves, and I was conscious of much pleasure in seeing them. One is shown over many a house in these days where the interest may be more complex, but not more definite.

'Those were her best things, poor dear,' said Elijah as he locked the door again. 'She told me that last summer before she was taken away that she couldn't think o' anything more she wanted, there was everything in the house, an' all her rooms was furnished pretty. I was goin' over to the Port, an' inquired for errands. I used to ask her to say what she wanted, cost or no cost – she was a very reasonable woman, an' 't was the place where she done all but her extra shopping. It kind o' chilled me up when she spoke so satisfied.'

'You don't go out fishing after Christmas?' I asked, as we came back to the bright kitchen.

'No; I take stiddy to my knitting after January sets in,' said the old seafarer. "T ain't worth while, fish make off into deeper water an' you can't stand no such perishin' for the sake o' what you get. I leave out a few traps in sheltered coves an' do a little lobsterin' on fair days. The young fellows braves it out, some on 'em; but, for me, I lay in my winter's yarn an' set here where 't is warm, an' knit an' take my comfort. Mother learnt me once when I was a lad; she was a beautiful knitter herself. I was laid up with a bad knee, an' she said 't would take up my time an' help her; we was a large family. They'll buy all the folks can do down here to Addicks' store. They say our Dunnet stockin's is gettin' to be celebrated up to Boston,– good quality o' wool an' even knittin' or somethin'. I've always been called a pretty hand to do nettin', but seines is master cheap to what they used to be when they was all hand worked. I change off to nettin' long towards spring, and I piece up my trawls and lines and get my fishin' stuff to rights. Lobster pots they require attention, but I make 'em up in spring weather when it's warm there in the barn. No; I ain't one o' them that likes to set an' do nothin'.

'You see the rugs, poor dear did them; she wa'n't very partial to knittin',' old Elijah went on, after he had counted his stitches. 'Our rugs is beginnin' to show wear, but I can't master none o' them womanish tricks. My sister, she tinkers 'em up. She said last time she was here that she guessed they'd last my time.'

'The old ones are always the prettiest,' I said.

'You ain't referrin' to the braided ones now?' answered Mr. Tilley. 'You see ours is braided for the most part, an' their good looks is all in the beginnin'. Poor dear used to say they made an easier floor. I go shufflin' round the house same's if 't was a bo't, and I always used to be stubbin' up the corners o' the hooked kind. Her an' me was always havin' our jokes together same's a boy an' girl. Outsiders never'd know nothin' about it to see us. She had nice manners with all, but to me there was nobody so entertainin'. She'd take off anybody's natural talk winter evenin's when we set here alone, so you'd think 't was them a-speakin'. There, there!'

I saw that he had dropped a stitch again, and was snarling the blue yarn round his clumsy fingers. He handled it and threw it off at arm's length as if it were a cod line; and frowned impatiently, but I saw a tear shining on his cheek.

I said that I must be going, it was growing late, and asked if I might come again, and if he would take me out to the fishing grounds some day.

'Yes, come any time you want to,' said my host, ' 't ain't so pleasant as when poor dear was here. Oh, I didn't want to lose her an' she didn't want to go, but it had to be. Such things ain't for us to say; there's no yes an' no to it.'

'You find Almiry Todd one o' the best o' women?' said Mr. Tilley as we parted. He was standing in the doorway and I had started off down the narrow green field. 'No, there ain't a better hearted woman in the State o' Maine. I've known her from a girl. She's had the best o' mothers. You tell her I'm liable to fetch her up a couple or three nice good mackerel early to-morrow,' he said. 'Now don't let it slip your mind. Poor dear, she always thought a sight o' Almiry, and she used to remind me there was nobody to fish for her; but I don't rec'lect it as I ought to. I see you drop a line yourself very handy now an' then.'

We laughed together like the best of friends, and I

spoke again about the fishing grounds, and confessed that I had no fancy for a southerly breeze and a ground swell.

'Nor me neither,' said the old fisherman. 'Nobody likes 'em, say what they may. Poor dear was disobliged by the mere sight of a bo't. Almiry's got the best o' mothers, I expect you know; Mis' Blackett out to Green Island; and we was always plannin' to go out when summer come; but there, I couldn't pick no day's weather that seemed to suit her just right. I never set out to worry her neither, 't wa'n't no kind o' use; she was so pleasant we couldn't have no fret nor trouble. 'T was never "you dear an' you darlin'" afore folks, an' "you divil" behind the door!'

As I looked back from the lower end of the field I saw him standing, a lonely figure in the doorway. 'Poor dear,' I repeated to myself half aloud; 'I wonder where she is and what she knows of the little world she left. I wonder what she has been doing these eight years!'

I gave the message about the mackerel to Mrs. Todd.

'Been visitin' with 'Lijah?' she asked with interest. 'I expect you had kind of a dull session; he ain't the talkin' kind; dwellin' so much long o' fish seems to make 'em lose the gift o' speech.' But when I told her that Mr. Tilley had been talking to me that day, she interrupted me quickly.

'Then 't was all about his wife, an' he can't say

nothin' too pleasant neither. She was modest with strangers, but there ain't one o' her old friends can ever make up her loss. For me, I don't want to go there no more. There's some folks you miss and some folks you don't, when they're gone, but there ain't hardly a day I don't think o' dear Sarah Tilley. She was always right there; yes, you knew just where to find her like a plain flower. 'Lijah's worthy enough; I do esteem 'Lijah, but he's a ploddin' man.'

CHAPTER TWENTY-ONE

A Dunnet Shepherdess

*

I

EARLY one morning at Dunnet Landing, as if it were still night, I waked, suddenly startled by a spirited conversation beneath my window. It was not one of Mrs. Todd's morning soliloquies; she was not addressing her plants and flowers in words of either praise or blame. Her voice was declamatory though perfectly good-humoured, while the second voice, a man's, was of lower pitch and somewhat deprecating.

The sun was just above the sea, and struck straight across my room through a crack in the blind. It was a strange hour for the arrival of a guest, and still too soon for the general run of business, even in that tiny eastern haven where daybreak fisheries and early tides must often rule the day.

The man's voice suddenly declared itself to my sleepy ears. It was Mr. William Blackett's.

'Why, sister Almiry,' he protested gently, 'I don't need none o' your nostrums!'

'Pick me a small han'ful,' she commanded. 'No, no, a *small* han'ful, I said,– o' them large pennyr'yal sprigs! I go to all the trouble an' cossetin' of 'em just so as to have you ready to meet such occasions, an' last year, you may remember, you never stopped here at all the day you went up country. An' the frost come at last an' blacked it. I never saw any herb that so objected to gardin ground; might as well try to flourish may-flowers in a common front yard. There, you can come in now, an' set and eat what breakfast you've got patience for. I've found everything I want, an' I'll mash 'em up an' be all ready to put 'em on.'

I heard such a pleading note of appeal as the speakers went round the corner of the house, and my curiosity was so demanding, that I dressed in haste, and joined my friends a little later, with two unnoticed excuses of the beauty of the morning, and the early mail boat. William's breakfast had been slighted; he had taken his cup of tea and merely pushed back the rest on the kitchen table. He was now sitting in a helpless con-dition by the side window, with one of his sister's purple calico aprons pinned close about his neck. Poor William was meekly submitting to being smeared, as to his countenance, with a most pungent and unat-tractive lotion of pennyroyal and other green herbs which had been hastily pounded and mixed with cream in the little white stone mortar.

I had to cast two or three straightforward looks at William to reassure myself that he really looked happy and expectant in spite of his melancholy cir-cumstances, and was not being overtaken by retribution. The brother and sister seemed to be on delightful terms with each other for once, and there was something of cheerful anticipation in their morning talk. I was reminded of Medea's anointing Jason before the great episode of the iron bulls, but to-day William really could not be going up country to see a railroad for the first time. I knew this to be one of his great schemes, but he was not fitted to appear in public, or to front an observing world of strangers. As I appeared he essayed to rise, but Mrs. Todd pushed him back into the chair.

'Set where you be till it dries on,' she insisted. 'Land sakes, you'd think he'd get over bein' a boy some time or 'nother, gettin' along in years as he is. An' you'd think he'd seen full enough o' fish, but once a year he has to break loose like this, an' travel off way up back o' the Bowden place – far out o' my beat, 't is – an' go a trout fishin'!'

Her tone of amused scorn was so full of challenge that William changed colour even under the green streaks.

'I want some change,' he said, looking at me and not at her. "T is the prettiest little shady brook you ever saw.'

'If he ever fetched home more'n a couple o' minnies, 't would seem worth while,' Mrs. Todd concluded, putting a last dab of the mysterious compound so perilously near her brother's mouth that William flushed again and was silent.

A little later I witnessed his escape, when Mrs. Todd had taken the foolish risk of going down cellar. There was a horse and waggon outside the garden fence, and presently we stood where we could see him driving up the hill with thoughtless speed. Mrs. Todd said nothing, but watched him affectionately out of sight.

'It serves to keep the mosquitoes off,' she said, and a moment later it occurred to my slow mind that she spoke of the pennyroyal lotion. 'I don't know sometimes but William's kind of poetical,' she continued, in her gentlest voice. 'You'd think if anything could cure him of it, 't would be the fish business.'

It was only twenty minutes past six on a summer morning, but we both sat down to rest as if the activities of the day were over. Mrs. Todd rocked gently for a time, and seemed to be lost, though not poorly, like Macbeth, in her thoughts. At last she resumed relations with her actual surroundings. 'I shall now put my lobsters on. They'll make us a good supper,' she announced. 'Then I can let the fire out for all day: give it a holiday, same's William. You can have a little one now, nice an' hot, if you ain't got all the breakfast you want. Yes, I'll put the lobsters on. William was very thoughtful to bring 'em over; William *is* thoughtful; if he only had a spark o' ambition, there be few could match him.'

This unusual concession was afforded a sympathetic listener from the depths of the kitchen closet. Mrs. Todd was getting out her old iron lobster pot, and began to speak of prosaic affairs. I hoped that I should hear something more about her brother and their island life, and sat idly by the kitchen window looking at the morning glories that shaded it, believing that some flaw of wind might set Mrs. Todd's mind on its former course. Then it occurred to me that she had spoken about our supper rather than our dinner, and I guessed that she might have some great scheme before her for the day.

When I had loitered for some time and there was no further word about William, and at last I was conscious of receiving no attention whatever, I went away. It was something of a disappointment to find that she put no hindrance in the way of my usual morning affairs, of going up to the empty little white schoolhouse on the hill where I did my task of writing. I had been almost sure of a holiday when I discovered that Mrs. Todd was likely to take one herself; we had not been far afield to gather herbs and pleasures for many days now, but a little later she had silently vanished. I found my luncheon ready on the table in the little entry, wrapped in its shining old homespun napkin, and as if by way of special consolation, there was a stone bottle of Mrs. Todd's best spruce beer, with a long piece of codline round it by which it could be lowered for coolness into the deep schoolhouse well.

I walked away with a dull supply of writing-paper and these provisions, feeling like a reluctant child who hopes to be called back at every step. There was no relenting voice to be heard, and when I reached the schoolhouse, I found that I had left an open window and a swinging shutter the day before, and the sea wind that blew at evening had fluttered my poor sheaf of papers all about the room.

So the day did not begin very well, and I began to

recognise that it was one of the days when nothing could be done without company. The truth was that my heart had gone trouting with William, but it would have been too selfish to say a word even to one's self about spoiling his day. If there is one way above another of getting so close to nature that one simply is a piece of nature, following a primeval instinct with perfect self-forgetfulness and forgetting everything except the dreamy consciousness of pleasant freedom, it is to take the course of a shady trout brook. The dark pools and the sunny shallows beckon one on; the wedge of sky between the trees on either bank, the speaking, companioning noise of the water, the amazing importance of what one is doing, and the constant sense of life and beauty make a strange transformation of the quick hours. I had a sudden memory of all this, and another, and another. I could not get myself free from 'fishing and wishing.'

At that moment I heard the unusual sound of wheels, and I looked past the high-growing thicket of wild-roses and straggling sumach to see the white nose and meagre shape of the Caplin horse; then I saw William sitting in the open waggon, with a small, expectant smile upon his face.

'I've got two lines,' he said. 'I was quite a piece up the road. I thought perhaps 'twas so you'd feel like going.'

There was enough excitement for most occasions in hearing William speak three sentences at once. Words seemed but vain to me at that bright moment. I stepped back from the schoolhouse window with a beating heart. The spruce-beer bottle was not yet in the well, and with that and my luncheon, and Pleasure at the helm, I went out into the happy world. The land breeze was blowing and, as we turned away, I saw a flutter of white go past the window as I left the schoolhouse and my morning's work to their neglected fate.

II

One seldom gave way to a cruel impulse to look at an ancient seafaring William, but one felt as if he were a growing boy; I only hope that he felt much the same about me. He did not wear the fishing clothes that belonged to his sea-going life, but a strangely shaped old suit of tea-coloured linen garments that might have been brought home years ago from Canton or Bombay. William had a peculiar way of giving silent assent when one spoke, but of answering your unspoken thoughts as if they reached him better than words. 'I find them very easy,' he said, frankly, referring to the clothes. 'Father had them in his old sea-chest.'

The antique fashion, a quaint touch of foreign grace and even imagination about the cut were very pleasing; if ever Mr. William Blackett had faintly resembled an old beau, it was upon that day. He now appeared to feel as if everything had been explained between us, as if everything were quite understood; and we drove for some distance without finding it necessary to speak again about anything. At last, when it must have been a little past nine o'clock, he stopped the horse beside a small farmhouse, and nodded when I asked if I should get down from the waggon. 'You can steer about north-east right across the pasture,' he said, looking from under the eaves of his hat with an expectant smile. 'I always leave the team here.'

I helped to unfasten the harness, and William led the horse away to the barn. It was a poor-looking little place, and a forlorn woman looked at us through the window before she appeared at the door. I told her that Mr. Blackett and I came up from the Landing to go fishing. 'He keeps a-comin', don't he?' she answered, with a funny little laugh, to which I was at a loss to find answer. When he joined us, I could not see that he took notice of her presence in any way, except to take an armful of dried salt fish from a corded stack in the back of the waggon which had been carefully covered with a piece of old sail. We had left a wake of their pungent flavour behind us all the way. I wondered what was going to become of the rest of them, and some fresh lobsters which were also disclosed to view, but he laid the present gift on the doorstep without a word, and a few minutes later, when I looked back as we crossed the pasture, the fish were being carried into the house.

I could not see any signs of a trout brook until I came close upon it in the bushy pasture, and presently we struck into the low woods of straggling spruce and fir mixed into a tangle of swamp maples and alders which stretched away on either hand up and down stream. We found an open place in the pasture where some taller trees seemed to have been overlooked rather than spared. The sun was bright and hot by this time, and I sat down in the shade while William produced his lines and cut and trimmed us each a slender rod. I wondered where Mrs. Todd was spending the morning, and if later she would think that pirates had landed and captured me from the schoolhouse.

III

The brook was giving that live, persistent call to a listener that trout brooks always make; it ran with a free, swift current even here, where it crossed an apparently level piece of land. I saw two unpromising, quick barbel chase each other upstream from bank to bank as we solemnly arranged our hooks and sinkers. I felt that William's glances changed from anxiety to relief when he found that I was used to such gear; perhaps he felt that we must stay together if I could not bait my own hook, but we parted happily, full of a pleasing sense of companionship.

William had pointed me up the brook, but I chose to go down, which was only fair because it was his day, though one likes as well to follow and see where a brook goes as to find one's way to the places it comes from, and its tiny springs and headwaters, and in this case trout were not to be considered. William's only real anxiety was lest I might suffer from mosquitoes. His own complexion was still strangely impaired by its defences, but I kept forgetting it, and looking to see if we were treading fresh pennyroyal underfoot, so efficient was Mrs. Todd's remedy. I was conscious, after we parted, and I turned to see if he were already fishing, and saw him wave his hand gallantly as he went away, that our friendship had made a great gain.

The moment that I began to fish the brook, I had a sense of its emptiness; when my bait first touched the water and went lightly down the quick stream, I knew that there was nothing to lie in wait for it. It is the same certainty that comes when one knocks at the door of an empty house, a lack of answering consciousness and of possible response; it is quite different if there is any life within. But it was a lovely brook, and I went a long way through woods and breezy open pastures, and found a forsaken house and overgrown farm, and laid up many pleasures for future joy and remembrance. At the end of the morning I came back to our meeting-place hungry and without any fish. William was already waiting, and we did not mention the matter of trout. We ate our luncheons with good appetites, and William brought our two stone bottles of spruce beer from the deep place in the brook where he had left them cool. Then we sat awhile longer in peace and quietness on the green banks.

As for William, he looked more boyish than ever, and kept a more remote and juvenile sort of silence. Once I wondered how he had come to be so curiously wrinkled, forgetting, absent-mindedly, to recognise the effects of time. He did not expect anyone else to keep up a vain show of conversation, and so I was silent as well as he. I glanced at him now and then, but I watched the leaves tossing against the sky and the red cattle moving in the pasture. 'I don't know's we need head for home. It's early yet,' he said at last, and I was as startled as if one of the gray firs had spoken.

'I guess I'll go up-along and ask after Thankful Hight's folks,' he continued. 'Mother'd like to get word '; and I nodded a pleased assent.

IV

William led the way across the pasture, and I followed with a deep sense of pleased anticipation. I do not believe that my companion had expected me to make any objection, but I knew that he was gratified by the easy way that his plans for the day were being seconded. He gave a look at the sky to see if there were any portents, but the sky was frankly blue; even the doubtful morning haze had disappeared.

We went northward along a rough, clayey road, across a bare-looking, sunburnt country full of tiresome long slopes where the sun was hot and bright, and I could not help observing the forlorn look of the farms. There was a good deal of pasture, but it looked deserted, and I wondered afresh why the people did not raise more sheep when that seemed the only possible use to make of their land. I said so to Mr. Blackett, who gave me a look of pleased surprise.

'That's what She always maintains,' he said eagerly. 'She's right about it too; well, you'll see!' I was glad to find myself approved, but I had not the least idea whom he meant, and waited until he felt like speaking again.

A few minutes later we drove down a steep hill and entered a large tract of dark spruce woods. It was delightful to be sheltered from the afternoon sun, and when we had gone some distance in the shade, to my great pleasure William turned the horse's head toward some bars, which he let down, and I drove through into one of those narrow, still, sweet-scented byways which seem to be paths rather than roads. Often we had to put aside the heavy drooping branches which barred the way, and once, when a sharp twig struck William in the face, he announced with such spirit that somebody ought to go through there with an axe, that I felt unexpectedly guilty. So far as I now remember, this was William's only remark all the way through the woods to Thankful Hight's folks, but from time to time he pointed or nodded at something which I might have missed: a sleepy little owl snuggled into the bend of a branch, or a tall stalk of cardinal flowers where the sunlight came down at the edge of a small, bright piece of marsh. Many times, being used to the company of Mrs. Todd and other friends who were in the habit of talking, I came near making an idle remark to William, but I was for the most part happily preserved; to be with him only for a short time was to live on a different level, where thoughts served best because they were thoughts in common; the primary effect upon our minds of the simple things and beauties that we saw. Once when I caught sight of a lovely gay pigeon woodpecker eyeing us curiously from a dead branch, and instinctively turned toward William, he gave an indulgent, comprehending nod which silenced me all the rest of the way. The wood-road was not a place for common, noisy conversation; one would interrupt the birds and all the still little beasts that belonged there. But it was mortifying to find how strong the habit of idle speech may become in one's self. One need not always be saying something in this noisy world. I grew conscious of the difference between William's usual fashion of life and mine; for him there were long days of silence in a sea-going boat, and I could believe that he and his mother usually spoke very little because they so perfectly understood each other. There was something peculiarly unresponding about their quiet island in the sea, solidly fixed into the still foundations of the world, against whose rocky shores the sea beats and calls and is unanswered.

We were quite half an hour going through the woods; the horse's feet made no sound on the brown, soft track under the dark evergreens. I thought that we should come out at last into more pastures, but there was no half-wooded strip of land at the end; the high woods grew squarely against an old stone wall and a sunshiny open field, and we came out suddenly into broad daylight that startled us and even startled the horse, who might have been napping as he walked, like an old soldier. The field sloped up to a low unpainted house that faced the east. Behind it were long, frost-whitened ledges that made the hill, with strips of green turf and bushes between. It was the wildest, most Titanic sort of pasture country up there; there was a sort of daring in putting a frail wooden house before it, though it might have the homely field and honest woods to front against. You thought of the elements and even of possible volcanoes as you looked up the stony heights. Suddenly I saw that a region of what I had thought gray stones was slowly moving, as if the sun was making my eyesight unsteady.

'There's the sheep!' exclaimed William, pointing eagerly. 'You see the sheep?' and sure enough, it was a great company of woolly backs, which seemed to have taken a mysterious protective resemblance to the ledges themselves. I could discover but little chance for pasturage on that high sunburnt ridge, but the sheep were moving steadily in a satisfied way as they fed along the slopes and hollows.

'I never have seen half so many sheep as these, all summer long!' I cried with admiration.

'There ain't so many,' answered William soberly. 'It's a great sight. They do so well because they're shepherded, but you can't beat sense into some folks.'

'You mean that somebody stays and watches them?' I asked.

'She observed years ago in her readin' that they don't turn out their flocks without protection anywhere but in the State o' Maine,' returned William. 'First thing that put it into her mind was a little old book mother's got; she read it one time when she come out to the Island. They call it the *Shepherd o' Salisbury Plain*. 'T wasn't the purpose o' the book to most, but when she read it, "There, Mis' Blackett!" she said, "that's where we've all lacked sense; our Bibles ought to have taught us that what sheep need is a shepherd." You see most folks about here gave up sheep-raisin' years ago 'count o' the dogs. So she gave up school-teachin' and went out to tend her flock, and has shepherded ever since, an' done well.'

For William, this approached an oration. He spoke with enthusiasm, and I shared the triumph of the moment. 'There she is now!' he exclaimed, in a different tone, as the tall figure of a woman came following the flock and stood still on the ridge, looking toward us as if her eyes had been quick to see a strange object in the familiar emptiness of the field. William stood up in the waggon, and I thought he was going to call or wave his hand to her, but he sat down again more clumsily than if the waggon had made the familiar motion of a boat, and we drove on toward the house.

It was a most solitary place to live, – a place where one might think that a life could hide itself. The thick woods were between the farm and the main road, and as one looked up and down the country, there was no other house in sight.

'Potatoes look well,' announced William. 'The old folks used to say that there wa'n't no better land out-doors than the Hight field.'

I found myself possessed of a surprising interest in the shepherdess, who stood far away in the hill pasture with her great flock, like a figure of Millet's high against the sky.

v

Everything about the old farmhouse was clean and orderly, as if the green dooryard were not only swept, but dusted. I saw a flock of turkeys stepping off carefully at a distance, but there was not the usual untidy flock of hens about the place to make everything look in disarray. William helped me out of the waggon as carefully as if I had been his mother, and nodded toward the open door with a reassuring look at me; but I waited until he had tied the horse and could lead the way, himself. He took off his hat just as we were going in, and stopped for a moment to smooth his thin gray hair with his hand, by which I saw that we had an affair of some ceremony. We entered an old-fashioned country kitchen, the floor scrubbed into unevenness and the doors well polished by the touch of hands. In a large chair facing the window there sat a masterful-looking old woman with the features of a warlike

191

Roman emperor, emphasised by a bonnet-like black cap with a band of green ribbon. Her sceptre was a palm-leaf fan.

William crossed the room toward her, and bent his head close to her ear.

'Feelin' pretty well to-day, Mis' Hight?' he asked, with all the voice his narrow chest could muster.

'No, I ain't, William. Here I have to set,' she answered coldly, but she gave an inquiring glance over his shoulder at me.

'This is the young lady who is stopping with Almiry this summer,' he explained, and I approached as if to give the countersign. She offered her left hand with considerable dignity, but her expression never seemed to change for the better. A moment later she said that she was pleased to meet me, and I felt as if the worst were over. William must have felt some apprehension, while I was only ignorant, as we had come across the field. Our hostess was more than disapproving, she was forbidding; but I was not long in suspecting that she felt the natural resentment of a strong energy that has been defeated by illness and made the spoil of captivity.

'Mother well as usual since you was up last year?' and William replied by a series of cheerful nods. The mention of dear Mrs. Blackett was a help to any conversation.

'Been fishin', ashore,' he explained, in a somewhat conciliatory voice. 'Thought you'd like a few for winter,' which explained at once the generous freight we had brought in the back of the waggon. I could see that the offering was no surprise, and that Mrs. Hight was interested.

'Well, I expect they're good as the last,' she said, but did not even approach a smile. She kept a straight, discerning eye upon me.

'Give the lady a cheer,' she admonished William, who hastened to place close by her side one of the straight-backed chairs that stood against the kitchen wall. Then he lingered for a moment like a timid boy. I could see that he wore a look of resolve, but he did not ask the permission for which he evidently waited.

'You can go search for Esther,' she said, at the end of a long pause that became anxious for both her guests. 'Esther'd like to see her'; and William in his pale nankeens disappeared with one light step and was off.

VI

'Don't speak too loud, it jars a person's head,' directed Mrs. Hight plainly. 'Clear an' distinct is what reaches me best. Any news to the Landin'?'

I was happily furnished with the particulars of a sudden death, and an engagement of marriage between a Caplin, a seafaring widower home from his voyage, and one of the younger Harrises; and now Mrs. Hight really smiled and settled herself in her chair. We exhausted one subject completely before we turned to the other. One of the returning turkeys took an unwarranted liberty, and, mounting the doorstep, came in and

walked about the kitchen without being observed by
its strict owner; and the tin dipper slipped off its nail
behind us and made an astonishing noise, and jar
enough to reach Mrs. Hight's inner ear and make her
turn her head to look at it; but we talked straight on.
We came at last to understand each other upon such
terms of friendship that she unbent her majestic port
and complained to me as any poor old woman might of
the hardships of her illness. She had already fixed
various dates upon the sad certainty of the year when
she had the shock, which had left her perfectly helpless
except for a clumsy left hand which fanned and ges-
tured, and settled and resettled the folds of her dress,
but could do no comfortable time-shortening work.

'Yes'm, you can feel sure I use it what I can,' she said
severely. "T was a long spell before I could let Esther
go forth in the mornin' till she'd got me up an' dressed
me, but now she leaves things ready overnight, and I
get 'em as I want 'em with my light pair o' tongs, and
I feel very able about helpin' myself to what I once did.
Then when Esther returns, all she has to do is to push
me out here into the kitchen. Some parts o' the year
Esther stays out all night, them moonlight nights when
the dogs are apt to be after the sheep, but she don't
use herself as hard as she once had to. She's well able
to hire somebody, Esther is, but there, you can't find
no hired man that wants to git up before five o'clock
nowadays; 't aint as 't was in my time. They're liable
to fall asleep too, and them moonlight nights she's so

anxious she can't sleep, and out she goes. There's a kind of a fold, she calls it, up there in a sheltered spot, and she sleeps up in a little shed she's got, — built it herself for lambin' time and when the poor foolish creaturs gets hurt or anything. I've never seen it, but she says it's in a lovely spot and always pleasant in any weather. You see off, other side of the ridge, to the south'ard, where there's houses. I used to think some time I'd get up to see it again, and all them spots she lives in, but I shan't now. I'm beginnin' to go back; an' 't aint surprisin'. I've kind of got used to disappointments,' and the poor soul drew a deep sigh.

VII

It was long before we noticed the lapse of time; I not only told every circumstance known to me of recent events among the households of Mrs. Todd's neighbourhood at the shore, but Mrs. Hight became more and more communicative on her part, and went carefully into the genealogical descent and personal experience of many acquaintants, until between us we had pretty nearly circumnavigated the globe and reached Dunnet Landing from an opposite direction to that in which we had started. It was long before my own interest began to flag; there was a flavour of the best sort in her definite and descriptive fashion of speech. It may be only a fancy of my own that in the sound and value of many words, with their lengthened vowels and doubled cadences, there is some faint survival on the Maine coast of the sound of English speech of Chaucer's time.

At last Mrs. Thankful Hight gave a suspicious look through the window.

'Where do you suppose they be?' she asked me. 'Esther must ha' been off to the far edge o' everything. I doubt William ain't been able to find her; can't he hear their bells? His hearin's all right?'

William had heard some herons that morning which were almost beyond the reach of my own ears, and almost beyond eyesight in the upper skies, and I told her so. I was luckily preserved by some unconscious instinct from saying that we had seen the shepherdess so near as we crossed the field. Unless she had fled faster than Atalanta, William must have been but a few minutes in reaching her immediate neighbourhood. I now discovered with a quick leap of amusement and delight in my heart that I had fallen upon a serious chapter of romance. The old woman looked suspiciously at me, and I made a dash to cover with a new piece of information; but she listened with lofty indifference, and soon interrupted my eager statements.

'Ain't William been gone some considerable time?' she demanded, and then in a milder tone: 'The time has re'lly flown; I do enjoy havin' company. I set here alone a sight o' long days. Sheep is dreadful fools; I expect they heerd a strange step, and set right off through bush and brier, spite of all she could do. But William might have the sense to return, 'stead o'

searchin' about. I want to inquire of him about his
mother. What was you goin' to say? I guess you'll
have time to relate it.'

My powers of entertainment were on the ebb, but I
doubled my diligence and we went on for another half
hour at least with banners flying, but still William did
not reappear. Mrs. Hight frankly began to show
fatigue.

'Somethin's happened, an' he's stopped to help her,'
groaned the old lady, in the middle of what I had found
to tell her about a rumour of disaffection with the
minister of a town I merely knew by name in the weekly
newspaper to which Mrs. Todd subscribed. 'You step
to the door, dear, an' look if you can't see 'em.' I
promptly stepped, and once outside the house I looked
anxiously in the direction which William had taken.

To my astonishment I saw all the sheep so near that
I wonder we had not been aware in the house of every
bleat and tinkle. And there, within a stone's throw, on
the first long gray ridge that showed above the juniper,
were William and the shepherdess engaged in pleasant
conversation. At first I was provoked and then amused,
and a thrill of sympathy warmed my whole heart.
They had seen me and risen as if by magic; I had a
sense of being the messenger of Fate. One could almost
hear their sighs of regret as I appeared; they must have
passed a lovely afternoon. I hurried into the house with
the reassuring news that they were not only in sight
but perfectly safe, with all the sheep.

Mrs. Hight, like myself, was spent with conversation, and had ceased even the one activity of fanning herself. I brought a desired drink of water, and happily remembered some fruit that was left from my luncheon. She revived with splendid vigour, and told me the simple history of her later years since she had been smitten in the prime of her life by the stroke of paralysis, and her husband had died and left her alone with Esther and a mortgage on their farm. There was only one field of good land, but they owned a great region of sheep pasture and a little woodland. Esther had always been laughed at for her belief in sheep-raising when one by one their neighbours were giving up their flocks, and when everything had come to the point of despair she she had raised all the money and bought all the sheep she could, insisting that Maine lambs were as good as any, and that there was a straight path by sea to Boston market. And by tending her flock herself she had managed to succeed; she had made money enough to pay off the mortgage five years ago, and now what they did not spend was safe in the bank. 'It has been stubborn work, day and night, summer and winter, an' now she's beginnin' to get along in years,' said the old mother sadly. 'She's tended me 'long o' the sheep, an' she's been a good girl right along, but she ought to have been a teacher'; and Mrs. Hight sighed heavily and plied the fan again.

We heard voices and William and Esther entered; they did not know that it was so late in the afternoon. William looked almost bold, and oddly like a happy young man rather than an ancient boy. As for Esther, she might have been Jeanne d'Arc returned to her sheep, touched with age and gray with the ashes of a great remembrance. She wore the simple look of saint-hood and unfeigned devotion. My heart was moved by the sight of her plain sweet face, weatherworn and gentle in its looks, her thin figure in its close dress, and the strong hand that clasped a shepherd's staff, and I could only hold William in new reverence; this silent farmer-fisherman who knew, and he alone, the noble and patient heart that beat within her breast. I am not sure that they acknowledged even to themselves that they had always been lovers; they could not consent to anything so definite or pronounced; but they were happy in being together in the world. Esther was un-touched by the fret and fury of life; she had lived in sunshine and rain among her silly sheep, and been refined instead of coarsened, while her touching patience with a ramping old mother, stung by the sense of defeat and mourning her lost activities, had given back a lovely self-possession, and habit of sweet temper. I had seen enough of old Mrs. Hight to know that nothing a sheep might do could vex a person who was used to the uncertainties and severities of her companionship.

IX

Mrs. Hight told her daughter at once that she had enjoyed a beautiful call, and got a great many new things to think of. This was said so frankly in my hearing that it gave a consciousness of high reward, and I was indeed recompensed by the grateful look in Esther's eyes. We did not speak much together, but we understood each other. For the poor old woman did not read, and could not sew or knit with her helpless hand, and they were far from any neighbours, while her spirit was as eager in age as in youth, and expected even more from a disappointing world. She had lived to see the mortgage paid and money in the bank, and Esther's success acknowledged on every hand, and there were still a few pleasures left in life. William had his mother, and Esther had hers, and they had not seen each other for a year, though Mrs. Hight had spoken of a year's making no change in William even at his age. She must have been in the far eighties herself, but of a noble courage and persistence in the world she ruled from her stiff-backed rocking-chair.

William unloaded his gift of dried fish, each one chosen with perfect care, and Esther stood by, watching him, and then she walked across the field with us beside the waggon. I believed that I was the only one who knew their happy secret, and she blushed a little as we said good-bye.

'I hope you ain't goin' to feel too tired, mother's so

deaf; no, I hope you won't be tired,' she said kindly, speaking as if she well knew what tiredness was. We could hear the neglected sheep bleating on the hill in the next moment's silence. Then she smiled at me, a smile of noble patience, of uncomprehended sacrifice, which I can never forget. There was all the remembrance of disappointed hopes, the hardships of winter, the loneliness of single-handedness in her look, but I understood, and I love to remember her worn face and her young blue eyes.

'Good-bye, William,' she said gently, and William said good-bye, and gave her a quick glance, but he did not turn to look back, though I did, and waved my hand as she was putting up the bars behind us. Nor did he speak again until we had passed through the dark woods and were on our way homeward by the main road. The grave yearly visit had been changed from a hope into a happy memory.

'You can see the sea from the top of her pasture hill,' said William at last.

'Can you?' I asked with surprise.

'Yes, it's very high land; the ledges up there show very plain in clear weather from the top of our island, and there's a high upstandin' tree that makes a land-mark for the fishin' grounds.' And William gave a happy sigh.

When we had nearly reached the Landing, my companion looked over into the back of the waggon and saw that the piece of sailcloth was safe, with which he had covered the dried fish. 'I wish we had got some trout,' he said wistfully. 'They always appease Almiry, and make her feel 't was worth while to go.'

I stole a glance at William Blackett. We had not seen a solitary mosquito, but there was a dark stripe across his mild face, which might have been an old scar won long ago in battle.

CHAPTER TWENTY-TWO

The Queen's Twin

*

I

THE coast of Maine was in former years brought so near to foreign shores by its busy fleet of ships that among the older men and women one still finds a surprising proportion of travellers. Each seaward-stretching headland with its high-set houses, each island of a single farm, has sent its spies to view many a Land of Eshcol; one may see plain, contented old faces at the windows, whose eyes have looked at far-away ports and known the splendours of the Eastern world. They shame the easy voyager of the North Atlantic and the Mediterranean; they have rounded the Cape of Good Hope and braved the angry seas of Cape Horn in small wooden ships; they have brought up their hardy boys and girls on narrow decks; they were among the last of the Northmen's children to go adventuring to unknown shores. More than this one cannot give to a young State for its enlightenment; the sea captains and the captains' wives of Maine knew something of the wide world, and never mistook their native parishes for the whole instead of a part thereof; they knew not only Thomaston and Castine and Portland, but London and Bristol and Bordeaux, and the strange-mannered harbours of the China Sea.

One September day, when I was nearly at the end

of my summer at Dunnet Landing, Mrs. Todd came home from a long, solitary stroll in the wild pastures, with an eager look as if she were just starting on a hopeful quest instead of returning. She brought a little basket with blackberries enough for supper, and held it towards me so that I could see that there were also some late and surprising raspberries sprinkled on top, but she made no comment upon her wayfaring. I could tell plainly that she had something very important to say.

'You haven't brought home a leaf of anything,' I ventured to this practised herb-gatherer. 'You were saying yesterday that the witch hazel might be in bloom.'

'I daresay, dear,' she answered in a lofty manner; 'I ain't goin' to say it wasn't; I ain't much concerned either way 'bout the facts o' witch hazel. Truth is, I've been off visitin'; there's an old Indian footpath leadin' over towards the Back Shore through the great heron swamp that anybody can't travel over all summer. You have to seize your time some day just now, while the low ground's summer-dried as it is to-day, and before the fall rains set in. I never thought of it till I was out o' sight o' home, and I says to myself, "To-day's the day, certain!" and stepped along smart as I could. Yes, I've been visitin'. I did get into one spot that was wet underfoot before I noticed; you wait till I get me a pair o' dry woollen stockings, in case of cold, and I'll come an' tell ye.'

Mrs. Todd disappeared. I could see that something had deeply interested her. She might have fallen in with either the sea-serpent or the lost tribes of Israel, such was her air of mystery and satisfaction. She had been away since just before mid-morning, and as I sat waiting by my window I saw the last red glow of autumn sunshine flare along the gray rocks of the shore and leave them cold again, and touch the far sails of some coastwise schooners so that they stood like golden houses on the sea.

I was left to wonder longer than I liked. Mrs. Todd was making an evening fire and putting things in train for supper; presently she returned, still looking warm and cheerful after her long walk.

'There's a beautiful view from a hill over where I've been,' she told me; 'yes, there's a beautiful prospect of land and sea. You wouldn't discern the hill from any distance, but 'tis the pretty situation of it that counts. I sat there a long spell, and I did wish for you. No, I didn't know a word about goin' when I set out this morning' (as if I had openly reproached her!); 'I only felt one o' them travellin' fits comin' on, an' I ketched up my little basket; I didn't know but I might turn and come back time for dinner. I thought it wise to set out your luncheon for you in case I didn't. Hope you had all you wanted; yes, I hope you had enough.'

'Oh, yes, indeed,' said I. My landlady was always peculiarly bountiful in her supplies when she left me to fare for myself, as if she made a sort of peace-offering or affectionate apology.

'You know that hill with the old house right on top over beyond the heron swamp? You'll excuse me for explainin',' Mrs. Todd began, 'but you ain't so apt to strike inland as you be to go right along shore. You know that hill; there's a path leadin' right over to it that you have to look sharp to find nowadays; it belonged to the up-country Indians when they had to make a carry to the landing here to get to the out' islands. I've heard the old folks say that there used to be a place across a ledge where they'd worn a deep track with their moccasin feet, but I never could find it. 'T is so overgrown in some places that you keep losin' the path in the bushes and findin' it as you can; but it runs pretty straight considerin' the lay o' the land, and I keep my eye on the sun and the moss that grows one side o' the tree trunks. Some brook's been choked up and the swamp's bigger than it used to be. Yes; I did get in deep enough, one place!'

I showed the solicitude that I felt. Mrs. Todd was no longer young, and in spite of her strong, great frame and spirited behaviour, I knew that certain ills were apt to seize upon her and would end some day by leaving her lame and ailing.

'Don't you go to worryin' about me,' she insisted, 'settin' still's the only way the Evil One'll ever get the upper hand o' me. Keep me movin' enough, an' I'm twenty year old summer an' winter both. I don't know why 't is, but I've never happened to mention the one I've been to see. I don't know why I never happened to speak the name of Abby Martin, for I often give her a thought, but 't is a dreadful out-o'-the-way place where she lives, and I haven't seen her myself for three or four years. She's a real good interesting woman, and we're well acquainted; she's nigher mother's age than mine, but she's very young feeling. She made me a nice cup o' tea, and I don't know but I should have stopped all night if I could have got word to you not to worry.'

Then there was a serious silence before Mrs. Todd spoke again to make a formal announcement.

'She is the Queen's Twin,' and Mrs. Todd looked steadily to see how I might bear the great surprise.

'The Queen's Twin?' I repeated.

'Yes, she's come to feel a real interest in the Queen, and anybody can see how natural 't is. They were born the very same day, and you would be astonished to see what a number o' other things have corresponded. She was speaking o' some o' the facts to me to-day, an' you'd think she'd never done nothing but read history. I see how earnest she was about it as I never did before. I've often and often heard her allude to the facts, but now she's got to be old and the hurry's over with her work, she's come to live a good deal in her thoughts, as folks often do, and I tell you 't is a sight o' company for her. If you want to hear about Queen Victoria, why Mis' Abby Martin 'll tell you everything. And the prospect from that hill I spoke of

is as beautiful as anything in this world; 't is worth while
your goin' over to see her just for that.'

'When can you go again?' I demanded eagerly.

'I should say to-morrow,' answered Mrs. Todd;
'yes, I should say to-morrow; but I expect 't would be
better to take one day to rest in between. I considered
that question as I was comin' home, but I hurried so
that there wa'n't much time to think. It's a dreadful
long way to go with a horse; you have to go 'most as
far as the old Bowden place an' turn off to the left, a
master long, rough road, and then you have to turn
right round as soon as you get there if you mean to get
home before nine o'clock at night. But to strike across
country from here, there's plenty o' time in the shortest
day, and you can have a good hour or two's visit beside;
't ain't but a very few miles, and it's pretty all the way
along. There used to be a few good families over
there, but they've died and scattered, so now she's far
from neighbours. There, she really cried, she was so
glad to see anybody comin'. You'll be amused to hear
her talk about the Queen, but I thought twice or three
times as I set there 't was about all the company she'd
got.'

'Could we go day after to-morrow?' I asked eagerly.

"T would suit me exactly,' said Mrs. Todd.

II

One can never be so certain of good New England
weather as in the days when a long easterly storm has

blown away the warm late-summer mists, and cooled
the air so that, however bright the sunshine is by day,
the nights come nearer and nearer to frostiness. There
was a cold freshness in the morning air when Mrs. Todd
and I locked the house-door behind us; we took the
key of the fields into our own hands that day, and put
out across country as one puts out to sea. When we
reached the top of the ridge behind the town it seemed
as if we had anxiously passed the harbour bar and were
comfortably in open sea at last.

'There now!' proclaimed Mrs. Todd, taking a long
breath, 'now I do feel safe. It's just the weather that's
liable to bring somebody to spend the day; I've had a
feeling of Mis' Elder Caplin from North Point bein'
close upon me ever since I waked up this mornin', an'
I didn't want to be hampered with our present plans.
she's a great hand to visit; she'll be spendin' the day
somewhere from now till Thanksgivin', but there's
plenty o' places at the Landin' where she goes, an' if I
ain't there she'll just select another. I thought mother
might be in, too, 't is so pleasant; but I run up the road
to look off this mornin' before you was awake, and
there was no sign o' the boat. If they hadn't started by
that time they wouldn't start, just as the tide is now; besides, I see a lot o' mackerel-men headin' Green Island
way, and they'll detain William. No, we're safe now,
an' if mother should be comin' in to-morrow we'll
have all this to tell her. She an' Mis' Abby Martin's
very old friends.'

We were walking down the long pasture slopes towards the dark woods and thickets of the low ground. They stretched away northward like an unbroken wilderness; the early mists still dulled much of the colour and made the uplands beyond look like a very far-off country.

'It ain't so far as it looks from here,' said my companion reassuringly, 'but we've got no time to spare either,' and she hurried on, leading the way with a fine sort of spirit in her step; and presently we struck into the old Indian footpath, which could be plainly seen across the long-unploughed turf of the pastures, and followed it among the thick, low-growing spruces. There the ground was smooth and brown underfoot, and the thin-stemmed trees held a dark and shadowy roof overhead. We walked a long way without speaking; sometimes we had to push aside the branches, and sometimes we walked in a broad aisle where the trees were larger. It was a solitary wood, birdless and beastless; there was not even a rabbit to be seen, or a crow high in air to break the silence.

'I don't believe the Queen ever saw such a lonesome trail as this,' said Mrs. Todd, as if she followed the thoughts that were in my mind. Our visit to Mrs. Abby Martin seemed in some strange way to concern the high affairs of royalty. I had just been thinking of English landscapes, and of the solemn hills of Scotland with their lonely cottages and stone-walled sheepfolds, and the wandering flocks on high cloudy pastures. I had often been struck by the quick interest and familiar allusion to certain members of the royal house which one found in distant neighbourhoods of New England; whether some old instincts of personal loyalty have survived all changes of time and national vicissitudes, or whether it is only that the Queen's own character and disposition have won friends for her so far away, it is impossible to tell. But to hear of a twin sister was the most surprising proof of intimacy of all, and I must confess that there was something remarkably exciting to the imagination in my morning walk. To think of being presented at Court in the usual way was for the moment quite commonplace.

III

Mrs. Todd was swinging her basket to and fro like a schoolgirl as she walked, and at this moment it slipped from her hand and rolled lightly along the ground as if there were nothing in it. I picked it up and gave it to her, whereupon she lifted the cover and looked in with anxiety.

"'T is only a few little things, but I don't want to lose 'em,' she explained humbly. "'T was lucky you took the other basket if I was goin' to roll it round. Mis' Abby Martin complained o' lacking some pretty pink silk to finish one o' her little frames, an' I thought I'd carry her some, and I had a bunch o' gold thread that had been in a box o' mine this twenty year. I never was one to do much fancy work, but we're all liable to be swept away by fashion. And then there's a small packet o' very choice herbs that I gave a good deal of attention to; they'll smarten her up and give her the best of appetites come spring. She was tellin' me that spring weather is very wiltin' an' trvin' to her, and she was beginnin' to dread it already. Mother's just the same way; if I could prevail on mother to take some o' these remedies in good season 't would make a world o' difference, but she gets all downhill before I have a chance to hear of it, and then William comes in to tell me, sighin' and bewailin', how feeble mother is. "Why can't you remember 'bout them good herbs that I never let her be without?" I say to him – he does provoke me so; and then off he goes, sulky enough, down to his boat. Next thing I know, she comes in to go to meetin', wantin' to speak to everybody and feelin' like a girl. Mis' Martin's case is very much the same; but she's nobody to watch her. William's kind o' slow-moulded; but there, any William's better than none when you get to be Mis' Martin's age.'

'Hadn't she any children?' I asked.

'Quite a number,' replied Mrs. Todd grandly, 'but some are gone and the rest are married and settled. She never was a great hand to go about visitin'. I don't know but Mis' Martin might be called a little peculiar. Even her own folks has to make company of her; she never slips in and lives right along with the rest as if 't was at home, even in her own children's houses. I heard one o' her sons' wives say once she'd much rather

have the Queen to spend the day if she could choose
between the two, but I never thought Abby was so
difficult as that. I used to love to have her come; she
may have been sort o' ceremonious, but very pleasant
and sprightly if you had sense enough to treat her her
own way. I always think she'd know just how to live
with great folks, and feel easier 'long of them an' their
ways. Her son's wife's a great driver with farm-work,
boards a great tableful o' men in hayin' time, an' feels
right in her element. I don't say but she's a good woman
an' smart, but sort o' rough. Anybody that's gentle
mannered an' precise like Mis' Martin would be a sort
o' restraint.

'There's all sorts o' folks in the country, same's there
is in the city,' concluded Mrs. Todd gravely, and I as
gravely agreed. The thick woods were behind us now,
and the sun was shining clear overhead, the morning
mists were gone, and a faint blue haze softened the
distance; as we climbed the hill where we were to see
the view, it seemed like a summer day. There was an
old house on the height, facing southward, – a mere
forsaken shell of an old house, with empty windows
that looked like blind eyes. The frost-bitten grass grew
close about it like brown fur, and there was a single
crooked bough of lilac holding its green leaves close by
the door.

'We'll just have a good piece of bread-an'-butter
now,' said the commander of the expedition, 'and then
we'll hang up the basket on some peg inside the house

out o' the way o' the sheep, and have a han'some entertainment as we're comin' back. She'll be all through
her little dinner when we get there, Mis' Martin will;
but she'll want to make us some tea, an' we must have
our visit an' be startin' back pretty soon after two. I
don't want to cross all that low ground again
after it's begun to grow chilly. An' it looks to me
as if the clouds might begin to gather late in the
afternoon.'

Before us lay a splendid world of sea and shore. The
autumn colours already brightened the landscape; and
here and there at the edge of a dark tract of pointed firs
stood a row of bright swamp-maples like scarlet flowers.
The blue sea and the great tide inlets were untroubled
by the lightest winds.

'Poor land, this is!' sighed Mrs. Todd as we sat down
to rest on the worn door-step. 'I've known three good
hard-workin' families that come here full o' hope an'
pride and tried to make something o' this farm, but it
beat 'em all. There's one small field that's excellent for
potatoes if you let half of it rest every year; but the
land's always hungry. Now, you see them little peaked
topped spruces an' fir balsams comin' up over the hill
all green an' hearty; they've got it all their own way!
Seems sometimes as if wild Natur' got jealous over a
certain spot, and wanted to do just as she'd a mind to.
You'll see here; she'll do her own ploughin' an' harrow-
in' with frost an' wet, an' plant just what she wants
and wait for her own crops. Man can't do nothin' with

it, try as he may. I tell you those little trees means business!'

I looked down the slope, and felt as if we ourselves were likely to be surrounded and overcome if we lingered too long. There was a vigour of growth, a persistence and savagery about the sturdy little trees that put weak human nature at complete defiance. One felt a sudden pity for the men and women who had been worsted after a long fight in that lonely place; one felt a sudden fear of the unconquerable, immediate forces of Nature, as in the irresistible moment of a thunderstorm.

'I can recollect the time when folks were shy o' these woods we just come through,' said Mrs. Todd seriously. 'The men-folks themselves never'd venture into 'em alone; if their cattle got strayed they'd collect whoever they could get, and start off all together. They said a person was liable to get bewildered in there alone, and in old times folks had been lost. I expect there was considerable fear left over from the old Indian times, and the poor days o' witchcraft; anyway, I've seen bold men act kind o' timid. Some women o' the Asa Bowden family went out one afternoon berryin' when I was a girl, and got lost and was out all night; they found 'em middle o' the mornin' next day, not half a mile from home, scared most to death, an' sayin' they'd heard wolves and other beasts sufficient for a caravan. Poor creatur's! they'd strayed at last into a kind of low place amongst some alders, an' one of 'em was so overset she

never got over it, an' went off in a sort o' slow decline.
'T was like them victims that drowns in a foot o' water;
but their minds did suffer dreadful. Some folks is born
afraid of the woods and all wild places, but I must say
they've always been like home to me.'

I glanced at the resolute, confident face of my companion. Life was very strong in her, as if some force
of Nature were personified in this simple-hearted
woman and gave her cousinship to the ancient deities.
She might have walked the primeval fields of Sicily;
her strong gingham skirts might at that very moment
bend the slender stalks of asphodel and be fragrant with
trodden thyme, instead of the brown wind-brushed
grass of New England and frost-bitten goldenrod. She
was a great soul, was Mrs. Todd, and I her humble
follower, as we went our way to visit the Queen's Twin,
leaving the bright view of the sea behind us, and de-
scending to a lower countryside through the dry pastures
and fields.

The farms all wore a look of gathering age, though
the settlement was, after all, so young. The fences were
already fragile, and it seemed as if the first impulse of
agriculture had soon spent itself without hope of renewal. The better houses were always those that had
some hold upon the riches of the sea; a house that
could not harbour a fishing-boat in some neighbouring
inlet was far from being sure of everyday comforts.
The land alone was not enough to live upon in that
stony region; it belonged by right to the forest, and to

the forest it fast returned. From the top of the hill where we had been sitting we had seen prosperity in the dim distance, where the land was good and the sun shone upon fat barns, and where warm-looking houses with three or four chimneys apiece stood high on their solid ridge above the bay.

As we drew nearer to Mrs. Martin's, it was sad to see what poor bushy fields, what thin and empty dwelling-places had been left by those who had chosen this disappointing part of the northern country for their home. We crossed the last field and came into a narrow rain-washed road, and Mrs. Todd looked eager and expectant and said that we were almost at our journey's end. 'I do hope Mis' Martin'll ask you into her best room where she keeps all the Queen's pictures. Yes, I think likely she will ask you; but 't ain't every-body she deems worthy to visit 'em, I can tell you!' said Mrs. Todd warningly. 'She's been collectin' 'em an' cuttin' 'em out o' newspapers an' magazines time out o' mind, and if she heard of anybody sailin' for an English port she'd contrive to get a little money to 'em and ask to have the last likeness there was. She's most covered her best-room wall now; she keeps that room shut up sacred as a meetin'-house! "I won't say but I have my favourites amongst 'em," she told me t'other day, "but they're all beautiful to me as they can be!" And she's made some kind o' pretty little frames for 'em all — you know there's always a new fashion o' frames comin' round; first 'twas shell-work, and then

217

'twas pine-cones, and bead-work's had its day, and now she's much concerned with perforated cardboard worked with silk. I tell you that best room's a sight to see! But you mustn't look for anything elegant,' continued Mrs. Todd, after a moment's reflection. 'Mis' Martin's always been in very poor, strugglin' circumstances. She had ambition for her children, though they took right after their father, an' had little for themselves; she wa'n't over an' above well married, however kind she may see fit to speak. She's been patient an' hard-workin' all her life, and always high above makin' mean complaints of other folks. I expect all this business about the Queen has buoyed her over many a shoal place in life. Yes, you might say that Abby'd been a slave, but there ain't any slave but has some freedom.'

IV

Presently I saw a low gray house standing on a grassy bank close to the road. The door was at the side, facing us, and a tangle of snowberry bushes and cinnamon roses grew to the level of the window-sills. On the doorstep stood a bent-shouldered, little old woman; there was an air of welcome and of unmistakable dignity about her.

'She sees us coming,' exclaimed Mrs. Todd in an excited whisper. 'There, I told her I might be over this way again if the weather held good, and if I came I'd bring you. She said right off she'd take great pleasure in havin' a visit from you; I was surprised, she's usually so retirin'.'

Even this reassurance did not quell a faint apprehension on our part; there was something distinctly formal in the occasion, and one felt that consciousness of inadequacy which is never easy for the humblest pride to bear. On the way I had torn my dress in an unexpected encounter with a little thornbush, and I could now imagine how it felt to be going to Court and forgetting one's feathers or her Court train.

The Queen's Twin was oblivious of such trifles; she stood waiting with a calm look until we came near enough to take her kind hand. She was a beautiful old woman, with clear eyes and a lovely quietness and genuineness of manner; there was not a trace of anything pretentious about her, or high-flown, as Mrs. Todd would say comprehensively. Beauty in age is rare enough in women who have spent their lives in the hard work of a farmhouse; but autumnlike and withered as this woman may have looked, her features had kept, or rather gained, a great refinement. She led us into her old kitchen and gave us seats, and took one of the little straight-backed chairs herself and sat a short distance away, as if she were giving audience to an ambassador. It seemed as if we should all be standing; you could not help feeling that the habits of her life were more ceremonious, but that for the moment she assumed the simplicities of the occasion.

Mrs. Todd was always Mrs. Todd, too great and

self-possessed a soul for any occasion to ruffle. I admired her calmness, and presently the slow current of neighbourhood talk carried one easily along; we spoke of the weather and the small adventures of the way, and then, as if I were after all not a stranger, our hostess turned almost affectionately to speak to me.

'The weather will be growing dark in London now. I expect that you've been in London, dear?' she said.

'Oh, yes,' I answered. 'Only last year.'

'It is a great many years since I was there, along in the forties,' said Mrs. Martin. ''T was the only voyage I ever made; most of my neighbours have been great travellers. My brother was master of a vessel, and his wife usually sailed with him; but that year she had a young child more frail than the others, and she dreaded the care of it at sea. It happened that my brother got a chance for my husband to go as supercargo, being a good accountant, and came one day to urge him to take it; he was very ill-disposed to the sea, but he had met with losses, and I saw my own opportunity and persuaded them both to let me go too. In those days they didn't object to a woman's being aboard to wash and mend, the voyages were sometimes very long. And that was the way I come to see the Queen.'

Mrs. Martin was looking straight in my eyes to see if I showed any genuine interest in the most interesting person in the world.

'Oh, I am very glad you saw the Queen,' I hastened

to say. 'Mrs. Todd has told me that you and she were born the very same day.'

'We were indeed, dear!' said Mrs. Martin, and she leaned back comfortably and smiled as she had not smiled before. Mrs. Todd gave a satisfied nod and glance, as if to say that things were going on as well as possible in this anxious moment.

'Yes,' said Mrs. Martin again, drawing her chair a little nearer, ''t was a very remarkable thing; we were born the same day, and at exactly the same hour, after you allowed for the difference in time. My father figured it out sea-fashion. Her Royal Majesty and I opened our eyes upon this world together; say what you may, 't is a bond between us.'

Mrs. Todd assented with an air of triumph, and untied her hat-strings and threw them back over her shoulders with a gallant air.

'And I married a man by the name of Albert, just the same as she did, and all by chance, for I didn't get the news that she had an Albert too till a fortnight afterward; news was slower coming then than it is now. My first baby was a girl, and I called her Victoria after my mate; but the next one was a boy, and my husband wanted the right to name him, and took his own name and his brother Edward's, and pretty soon I saw in the paper that the little Prince o' Wales had been christened just the same. After that I made excuse to wait till I I knew what she'd named her children. I didn't want to break the chain, so I had an Alfred, and my darling

Alice that I lost long before she lost hers, and there I stopped. If I'd only had a dear daughter to stay at home with me, same's her youngest one, I should have been so thankful! But if only one of us could have a little Beatrice, I'm glad 't was the Queen; we've both seen trouble, but she's had the most care.'

I asked Mrs. Martin if she lived alone all the year, and was told that she did except for a visit now and then from one of her grandchildren, 'the only one that really likes to come an' stay quiet 'long o' grandma. She always says quick as she's through her schoolin' she's goin' to live with me all the time, but she's very pretty an' has taking ways,' said Mrs. Martin, looking both proud and wistful, 'so I can tell nothing at all about it! Yes, I've been alone most o' the time since my Albert was taken away, and that's a great many years; he had a long time o' failing and sickness first.' (Mrs. Todd's foot gave an impatient scuff on the floor.) 'An' I've always lived right here. I ain't like the Queen's Majesty, for this is the only palace I've got,' said the dear old thing, smiling again. 'I'm glad of it too; I don't like changing about, an' our stations in life are set very different. I don't require what the Queen does, but sometimes I've thought 't was left to me to do the plain things she don't have time for. I expect she's a beautiful housekeeper, nobody couldn't have done better in her high place, and she's been as good a mother as she's been a queen.'

'I guess she has, Abby,' agreed Mrs. Todd instantly.

'How was it you happened to get such a good look at her? I meant to ask you again when I was here t'other day.'

'Our ship was layin' in the Thames, right there above Wapping. We was dischargin' cargo, and under orders to clear as quick as we could for Bordeaux to take on an excellent freight o' French goods,' explained Mrs. Martin eagerly. 'I heard that the Queen was goin' to a great review of her army, and would drive out o' her Buckin'ham Palace about ten o'clock in the mornin', and I run aft to Albert, my husband, and brother Horace, where they was standin' together by the hatchway, and told 'em they must one of 'em take me. They laughed, I was in such a hurry, and said they couldn't go; and I found they meant it and got sort of impatient when I began to talk, and I was 'most broken-hearted; 't was all the reason I had for makin' that hard voyage. Albert couldn't help often reproachin' me, for he did so resent the sea, an' I'd known how 't would be before we sailed; but I'd minded nothing all the way till then, and I just crep' back to my cabin an' begun to cry. They was disappointed about their ship's cook, an' I'd cooked for fo'c's'le an' cabin myself all the way over; 't was dreadful hard work, specially in rough weather; we'd had head winds an' a six weeks' voyage. They'd acted sort of ashamed o' me when I pled so to go ashore, an' that hurt my feelin's most of all. But Albert come below pretty soon; I'd never given way so in my life, an' he begun to act frightened, and treated me gentle just as he did when we was goin' to be married, an' when I got over sobbin' he went on deck and saw Horace an' talked it over what they could do; they really had their duty to the vessel, and couldn't be spared that day. Horace was real good when he understood everything, and he come an' told me I'd more than worked my passage an' was goin' to do just as I liked now we was in port. He'd engaged a cook, too, that was comin' aboard that mornin' and he was goin' to send the ship's carpenter with me – a nice fellow from up Thomaston way; he'd gone to put on his ashore clothes as quick's he could. So then I got ready, and we started off in the small boat and rowed up river. I was afraid we were too late, but the tide was setting up very strong, and we landed an' left the boat to a keeper, and I run all the way up those great streets and across a park. 'T was a great day, with sights o' folks everywhere, but 'twas just as if they was nothin' but wax images to me. I kep' askin' my way an' runnin' on with the carpenter comin' after as best he could, and just as I worked to the front o' the crowd by the palace, the gates were flung open and out she came; all prancin' horses and shinin' gold, and in a beautiful carriage there she sat; 't was a moment o' heaven to me. I saw her plain, and she looked right at me so pleasant and happy, just as if she knew there was somethin' different between us from other folks.'

There was a moment when the Queen's Twin could not go on and neither of her listeners could ask a question.

'Prince Albert was sitting right beside her in the carriage,' she continued. 'Oh, he was a beautiful man! Yes, dear, I saw 'em both together just as I see you now, and then she was gone out o' sight in another minute, and the common crowd was all spread over the place pushin' an' cheerin'. 'T was some kind o' holiday, an' the carpenter and I got separated, an' then I found him again after I didn't think I should, an' he was for makin' a day of it, and goin' to show me all the sights; he'd been in London before, but I didn't want nothin' else, an' we went back through the streets down to waterside an' took the boat. I remember I mended an old coat o' my Albert's as good as I could, sittin' on the quarter deck in the sun all that afternoon, and 't was all as if I was livin' in a lovely dream. I don't know how to explain it, but there hasn't been no friend I've felt so near to me ever since.'

One could not say much – only listen. Mrs. Todd put in a discerning question now and then, and Mrs. Martin's eyes shone brighter and brighter as she talked. What a lovely gift of imagination and true affection was in this fond old heart! I looked about the plain New England kitchen, with its wood-smoked walls and homely braided rugs on the worn floor, and all its simple furnishings. The loud-ticking clock seemed to encourage us to speak; at the other side of the room was an early newspaper portrait of Her Majesty the Queen of Great Britain and Ireland. On a shelf below were some flowers in a little glass dish, as if they were put before a shrine.

'If I could have had more to read, I should have known most everything about her,' said Mrs. Martin wistfully. 'I've made the most of what I did have, and thought it over and over till it came clear. I sometimes seem to have her all my own, as if we'd lived right together. I've often walked out into the woods alone and told her what my troubles was, and it always seemed as if she told me 't was all right, an' we must have patience. I've got her beautiful book about the Highlands; 't was dear Mrs. Todd here that found out about her printing it and got a copy for me, and it's been a treasure to my heart, just as if 't was written right to me. I always read it Sundays now, for my Sunday treat. Before that I used to have to imagine a good deal, but when I come to read her book, I knew what I expected was all true. We do think alike about so many things,' said the Queen's Twin with affectionate certainty. 'You see, there is something between us, being born just at the same time; 't is what they call a birthright. She's had great tasks put upon her, being the Queen, an' mine has been the humble lot; but she's done the best she could, nobody can say to the contrary, and there's something between us; she's been the great lesson I've had to live by. She's been everything to me. An' when she had her jubilee, oh, how my heart was with her!'

'There, 't wouldn't play the part in her life it has in mine,' said Mrs. Martin generously, in answer to something one of her listeners had said. 'Sometimes I think, now she's older, she might like to know about us.

When I think how few old friends anybody has left at our age, I suppose it may be just the same with her as it is with me; perhaps she would like to know how we came into life together. But I've had a great advantage in seeing her, an' I can always fancy her goin' on, while she don't know nothin' yet about me, except she may feel my love stayin' her heart sometimes an' not know just where it comes from. An' I dream about our being together out in some pretty fields, young as ever we was, and holdin' hands as we walk along. I'd like to know if she ever has that dream too. I used to have days when I made believe she did know, an' was comin' to see me,' confessed the speaker shyly, with a little flush on her cheeks; 'and I'd plan what I could have nice for supper, and I wasn't goin' to let anybody know she was here havin' a good rest, except I'd wish you, Almira Todd, or dear Mis' Blackett would happen in, for you'd know just how to talk with her. You see, she likes to be up in Scotland, right out in the wild country, better than she does anywhere else.'

'I'd really love to take her out to see mother at Green Island,' said Mrs. Todd with a sudden impulse.

'Oh, yes! I should love to have you,' exclaimed Mrs. Martin, and then she began to speak in a lower tone. 'One day I got thinkin' so about my dear Queen,' she said, 'an' livin' so in my thoughts, that I went to work an' got all ready for her, just as if she was really comin'. I never told this to a livin' soul before, but I feel you'll understand. I put my best fine sheets and blankets I spun an' wove myself on the bed, and I picked some pretty flowers and put 'em all round the house, an' I worked as hard an' happy as I could all day, and had as nice a supper ready as I could get, sort of telling myself a story all the time. She was comin' an' I was goin' to see her again, an' I kep' it up until nightfall; an' when I see the dark an' it come to me I was all alone, the dream left me, an' I sat down on the doorstep an' felt all foolish an' tired. An' if you'll believe it, I heard steps comin', an' an old cousin o' mine come wanderin' along, one I was apt to be shy of. She wasn't all there, as folks used to say, but harmless enough and a kind of poor old talking body. And I went right to meet her when I first heard her call, 'stead o' hidin' as I sometimes did, an' she come in dreadful willin', an' we sat down to supper together; 't was a supper I should have had no heart to eat alone.'

'I don't believe she ever had such a splendid time in her life as she did then. I heard her tell all about it afterwards,' exclaimed Mrs. Todd compassionately. 'There, now I hear all this it seems just as if the Queen might have known and couldn't come herself, so she sent that poor old creatur' that was always in need!'

Mrs. Martin looked timidly at Mrs. Todd and then at me. ''T was childish o' me to go an' get supper,' she confessed.

'I guess you wa'n't the first one to do that,' said Mrs. Todd. 'No, I guess you wa'n't the first one who's got supper that way, Abby,' and then for a moment she could say no more.

Mrs. Todd and Mrs. Martin had moved their chairs a little so that they faced each other, and I, at one side, could see them both.

'No, you never told me o' that before, Abby,' said Mrs. Todd gently. 'Don't it show that for folks that have any fancy in 'em, such beautiful dreams is the real part o' life? But to most folks the common things that happens outside 'em is all in all.'

Mrs. Martin did not appear to understand at first, strange to say, when the secret of her heart was put into words; then a glow of pleasure and comprehension shone upon her face. 'Why, I believe you're right, Almira!' she said, and turned to me.

'Wouldn't you like to look at my pictures of the Queen?' she asked, and we rose and went into the best room.

†

The midday visit seemed very short. September hours are brief to match the shortening days. The great subject was dismissed for a while after our visit to the Queen's pictures, and my companions spoke much of lesser persons until we drank the cup of tea which Mrs. Todd had foreseen. I happily remembered that the Queen herself is said to like a proper cup of tea, and this at once seemed to make her Majesty kindly join so remote and reverent a company. Mrs. Martin's thin cheeks took on a pretty colour like a girl's. 'Somehow I always have thought of her when I made it extra good,' she said. 'I've got a real china cup that belonged to my grandmother, and I believe I shall call it hers now.'

'Why don't you?' responded Mrs. Todd warmly, with a delightful smile.

Later they spoke of a promised visit which was to be made in the Indian summer to the Landing and Green Island, but I observed that Mrs. Todd presented the little parcel of dried herbs, with full directions, for a cure-all in the spring, as if there were no real chance of their meeting again first. As we walked back from the turn of the road the Queen's Twin was still standing on the doorstep watching us away, and Mrs. Todd stopped, and stood still for a moment before she waved her hand again.

'There's one thing certain, dear,' she said to me with great discernment; 'it ain't as if we left her all alone!'

Then we set out upon our long way home over the hill, where we lingered in the afternoon sunshine, and through the dark woods across the heron-swamp.

CHAPTER TWENTY-THREE

William's Wedding

✳

I

THE hurry of life in a large town, the constant putting aside of preference to yield to a most unsatisfactory activity, began to vex me, and one day I took the train, and only left it for the eastward-bound boat. Carlyle says somewhere that the only happiness a man ought to ask for is happiness enough to get his work done; and against this the complexity and futile ingenuity of social life seems a conspiracy. But the first salt wind from the east, the first sight of a lighthouse set boldly on its outer rock, the flash of a gull, the waiting procession of sea-ward-bound firs on an island, made me feel solid and definite again, instead of a poor, incoherent being. Life was resumed, and anxious living blew away as if it had not been. I could not breathe deep enough or long enough. It was a return to happiness.

The coast had still a wintry look; it was far on in May, but all the shore looked cold and sterile. One was conscious of going north as well as east, and as the day went on the sea grew colder, and all the warmer air and bracing strength and stimulus of the autumn weather, and storage of the heat of summer, were quite gone. I was very cold and very tired when I came at evening up the lower bay, and saw the white houses of Dunnet Landing climbing the hill. They had a friendly look, these little houses, not as if they were climbing up the shore, but as if they were rather all coming down to meet a fond and weary traveller, and I could hardly wait with patience to step off the boat. It was not the usual eager company on the wharf. The coming-in of the mail-boat was the one large public event of a summer day, and I was disappointed at seeing none of my intimate friends but Johnny Bowden, who had evidently done nothing all winter but grow, so that his short sea-smitten clothes gave him a look of poverty.

Johnny's expression did not change as we greeted each other, but I suddenly felt that I had shown indifference and inconvenient delay by not coming sooner; before I could make an apology he took my small portmanteau, and walking before me in his old fashion he made straight up the hilly road toward Mrs. Todd's. Yes, he was much grown – it had never occurred to me the summer before that Johnny was likely, with the help of time and other forces, to grow into a young man; he was such a well-framed and well-settled chunk of a boy that nature seemed to have set him aside as something finished, quite satisfactory, and entirely completed.

The wonderful little green garden had been enchanted away by winter. There were a few frost-bitten twigs and some thin shrubbery against the fence, but it was a most unpromising small piece of ground. My heart was beating like a lover's as I passed it on the way to the door of Mrs. Todd's house, which seemed to have become much smaller under the influence of winter weather.

'She hasn't gone away?' I asked Johnny Bowden with a sudden anxiety just as we reached the doorstep.

'Gone away!' he faced me with blank astonishment, – 'I see her settin' by Mis' Caplin's window, the one nighest the road, about four o'clock!' And eager with suppressed news of my coming, he made his entrance as if the house were a burrow.

Then on my homesick heart fell the voice of Mrs. Todd. She stopped, through what I knew to be excess of feeling, to rebuke Johnny for bringing in so much mud, and I dallied for one moment during the ceremony; then we met again face to face.

II

'I daresay you can advise me what shapes they are goin' to wear. My meetin'-bunnit ain't goin' to do me again this year; no! I can't expect 't would do me forever,' said Mrs. Todd, as soon as she could say anything. 'There! do set down and tell me how you have been! We've got a weddin' in the family, I s'pose you know?'

'A wedding!' said I, still full of excitement.

'Yes; I expect if the tide serves and the line storm don't overtake him they'll come in and appear out on Sunday. I shouldn't have concerned me about the bunnit for a month yet, nobody would notice, but havin' an occasion like this I shall show consider'ble. 'T will be an ordeal for William!'

'For *William!*' I exclaimed. 'What do you mean, Mrs. Todd?'

She gave a comfortable little laugh. 'Well, the Lord's seen reason at last an' removed Mis' Cap'n Hight up to the farm, an' I don't know but the weddin's goin' to be this week. Esther's had a great deal of business disposin' of her flock, but she's done extra well – the folks that owns the next place goin' up country are well off. 'T is elegant land north side o' that bleak ridge, an' one o' the boys has been Esther's right-hand man of late. She instructed him in all matters, and after she markets the early lambs he's goin' to take the farm on halves, an' she's give the refusal to him to buy her out within two years. She's reserved the buryin'-lot, an' the right o' way in, an' – '

I couldn't stop for details. I demanded reassurance of the central fact.

'William going to be married?' I repeated; whereat Mrs. Todd gave me a searching look that was not without scorn.

'Old Mis' Hight's funeral was a week ago Wednesday, and 't was very well attended,' she assured me after a moment's pause.

'Poor thing!' said I, with a sudden vision of her helplessness and angry battle against the fate of illness; 'it was very hard for her.'

'I thought it was hard for Esther!' said Mrs. Todd
without sentiment.

III

I had an odd feeling of strangeness: I missed the
garden, and the little rooms, to which I had added a
few things of my own the summer before, seemed
oddly unfamiliar. It was like the hermit crab in a cold
new shell, – and with the windows shut against the
raw May air, and a strange silence and grayness of the
sea all that first night and day of my visit, I felt as if I
had after all lost my hold of that quiet life.

Mrs. Todd made the apt suggestion that city persons
were prone to run themselves to death, and advised me
to stay and get properly rested now that I had taken the
trouble to come. She did not know how long I had been
homesick for the conditions of life at the Landing the
autumn before – it was natural enough to feel a little
unsupported by compelling incidents on my return.

Some one has said that one never leaves a place, or
arrives at one, until the next day! But on the second
morning I woke with the familiar feeling of interest
and ease, and the bright May sun was streaming in,
while I could hear Mrs. Todd's heavy footsteps pound-
ing about in the other part of the house as if something
were going to happen. There was the first golden
robin singing somewhere close to the house, and a
lovely aspect of spring now, and I looked at the garden
to see that in the warm night some of its treasures had

grown a hand's breadth; the determined spikes of yellow daffies stood tall against the doorsteps, and the bloodroot was unfolding leaf and flower. The belated spring which I had left behind farther south had overtaken me on this northern coast. I even saw a presumptuous dandelion in the garden border.

It is difficult to report the great events of New England; expression is so slight, and those few words which escape us in moments of deep feeling look but meagre on the printed page. One has to assume too much of the dramatic fervour as one reads; but as I came out of my room at breakfast-time I met Mrs. Todd face to face, and when she said to me, 'This weather'll bring William in after her; 't is their happy day!' I felt something take possession of me which ought to communicate itself to the least sympathetic reader of this cold page. It is written for those who have a Dunnet Landing of their own: who either kindly share this with the writer, or possess another.

'I ain't seen his comin' sail yet; he'll be likely to dodge round among the islands so he'll be the less observed,' continued Mrs. Todd. 'You can get a dory up the bay, even a clean new painted one, if you know as how, keepin' it against the high land.' She stepped to the door and looked off to sea as she spoke. I could see her eye follow the grey shores to and fro, and then a bright light spread over her calm face. 'There he comes, and he's strikin' right in across the open bay like a man!' she said with splendid approval. 'See, there he comes! Yes, there's William, and he's bent his new sail.'

I looked too, and saw the fleck of white no larger than a gull's wing yet, but present to her eager vision.

I was going to France for the whole long summer that year, and the more I thought of such an absence from these simple scenes the more dear and delightful they became. Santa Teresa says that the true proficiency of the soul is not in much thinking, but in much loving, and sometimes I believed that I had never found love in its simplicity as I had found it at Dunnet Landing in the various hearts of Mrs. Blackett and Mrs. Todd and William. It is only because one came to know them, these three, loving and wise and true, in their own habitations. Their counterparts are in every village in the world, thank heaven, and the gift to one's life is only in its discernment. I had only lived in Dunnet until the usual distractions and artifices of the world were no longer in control, and I saw these simple natures clear. 'The happiness of life is in its recognitions. It seems that we are not ignorant of these truths, and even that we believe them; but we are so little accustomed to think of them, they are so strange to us—'

'Well now, deary me!' said Mrs. Todd, breaking into exclamation; 'I've got to fly round—I thought he'd have to beat; he can't sail far on that tack, and he won't be in for a good hour yet — I expect he's made every arrangement, but he said he shouldn't go up after Esther unless the weather was good, and I declare it did look doubtful this morning.'

I remembered Esther's weather-worn face. She was like a Frenchwoman who had spent her life in the fields. I remembered her pleasant look, her child-like eyes, and thought of the astonishment of joy she would feel now in being taken care of and tenderly sheltered from wind and weather after all these years. They were going to be young again now, she and William, to forget work and care in the spring weather. I could hardly wait for the boat to come to land, I was so eager to see his happy face.

'Cake an' wine I'm goin' to set 'em out!' said Mrs. Todd. 'They won't stop to set down for an ordered meal, they'll want to get right out home quick's they can. Yes, I'll give 'em some cake an' wine — I've got a rare plum-cake from my best receipt, and a bottle o' wine that the old Cap'n Denton of all give me, one of two, the day I was married, one we had and one we saved, and I've never touched it till now. He said there wa'n't none like it in the State o' Maine.'

It was a day of waiting, that day of spring; the May weather was as expectant as our fond hearts, and one could see the grass grow green hour by hour. The warm air was full of birds, there was a glow of light on the sea instead of the cold shining of chilly weather

238

which had lingered late. There was a look on Mrs. Todd's face which I saw once and could not meet again. She was in her highest mood. Then I went out early for a walk, and when I came back we sat in different rooms for the most part. There was such a thrill in the air that our only conversation was in her most abrupt and incisive manner. She was knitting, I believe, and as for me I dallied with a book. I heard her walking to and fro, and, the door being wide open now, she went out and paced the front walk to the gate as if she walked a quarter-deck.

It is very solemn to sit waiting for the great events of life – most of us have done it again and again – to be expectant of life or expectant of death gives one the same feeling.

But at the last Mrs. Todd came quickly back from the gate, and standing in the sunshine at the door, she beckoned me as if she were a sibyl.

'I thought you comprehended everything the day you was up there,' she added with a little more patience in her tone, but I felt that she thought I had lost instead of gained since we parted the autumn before.

'William's made this pretext o' goin' fishin' for the last time. 'T wouldn't done to take notice, 't would 'a scared him to death! but there never was nobody took less comfort out o' forty years courtin'. No, he won't have to make no further pretexts,' said Mrs. Todd, with an air of triumph.

'Did you know where he was going that day?' I

asked, with a sudden burst of admiration at such discernment.

'I did!' replied Mrs. Todd grandly.

'Oh! but that pennyroyal lotion,' I indignantly protested, remembering that under pretext of mosquitoes she had besmeared the poor lover in an awful way – why, it was outrageous! Medea could not have been more conscious of high ultimate purposes.

'Darlin',' said Mrs. Todd, in the excitement of my arrival and the great concerns of marriage, 'he's got a beautiful shaped face, and they pison him very unusual – you wouldn't have had him present himself to his lady all lop-sided with a mosquito-bite? Once when we was young I rode up with him, and they set upon him in concert the minute we entered the woods.' She stood before me reproachfully, and I was conscious of deserved rebuke. 'Yes, you've come just in the nick of time to advise me about a bunnit. They say large bows on top is liable to be worn.'

IV

The period of waiting was one of direct contrast to these high moments of recognition. The very slowness of the morning hours wasted that sense of excitement with which we had begun the day. Mrs. Todd came down from the mount where her face had shone so bright, to the cares of common life, and some acquaintances from Black Island for whom she had little natural preference or liking came, bringing a poor, sickly child to get medical advice. They were noisy women, with harsh, clamorous voices, and they stayed a long time. I heard the clink of teacups, however, and could detect no impatience in the tones of Mrs. Todd's voice; but when they were at last going away, she did not linger unduly over her leave-taking, and returned to me to explain that they were people she had never liked, and they had made an excuse of a friendly visit to save their doctor's bill; but she pitied the poor little child, and knew beside that the doctor was away.

'I had to give 'em the remedies right out,' she told me; 'they wouldn't have bought a cent's worth o' drugs down to the store for that dwindlin' thing. She needed feedin' up, and I don't expect she gets milk enough; they're great butter-makers down to Black Island, 't is excellent pasturage, but they use no milk themselves, and their butter is heavy laden with salt to make weight, so that you'd think all their ideas come down from Sodom.'

She was very indignant and very wistful about the pale little girl. 'I wish they'd let me kept her,' she said. 'I kind of advised it, and her eyes was so wishful in that pinched face when she heard me, so that I could see what was the matter with her, but they said she wa'n't prepared. Prepared!' And Mrs. Todd sniffed like an offended war-horse, and departed; but I could hear her still grumbling and talking to herself in high dudgeon an hour afterward.

At the end of that time her arch enemy, Mari' Harris, appeared at the side-door with a gingham handkerchief over her head. She was always on hand for the news, and made some formal excuse for her presence,— she wished to borrow the weekly paper. Captain Littlepage, whose housekeeper she was, had taken it from the post-office in the morning, but had forgotten, being of failing memory, what he had done with it.

'How is the poor old gentleman?' asked Mrs. Todd with solicitude, ignoring the present errand of Maria and all her concerns.

I had spoken the evening before of intended visits to Captain Littlepage and Elijah Tilley, and I now heard Mrs. Todd repeating my inquiries and intentions, and fending off with unusual volubility of her own the curious questions that were sure to come. But at last Maria Harris secured an opportunity and boldly inquired if she had not seen William ashore early that morning.

'I don't say he wasn't,' replied Mrs. Todd; 'Thu'sday's a very usual day with him to come ashore.'

'He was all dressed up,' insisted Maria – she really had no sense of propriety. 'I didn't know but they was going to be married?'

Mrs. Todd did not reply. I recognised from the sounds that reached me that she had retired to the fastnesses of the kitchen-closet and was clattering the tins.

'I expect they'll marry soon anyway,' continued the visitor.

'I expect they will if they want to,' answered Mrs. Todd. 'I don't know nothin' 't all about it; that's what folks say.' And presently the gingham handkerchief retreated past my window.

'I routed her, horse and foot,' said Mrs. Todd proudly, coming at once to stand at my door. 'Who's comin' now?' as two figures passed inward bound to the kitchen.

They were Mrs. Begg and Johnny Bowden's mother, who were favourites, and were received with Mrs. Todd's usual civilities. Then one of the Mrs. Caplins came with a cup in hand to borrow yeast. On one pretext or another nearly all our acquaintances came to satisfy themselves of the facts, and see what Mrs. Todd would impart about the wedding. But she firmly avoided the subject through the length of every call and errand, and answered the final leading question of each curious guest with her noncommittal phrase, 'I don't know nothin' 't all about it; that's what folks say!'

She had just repeated this for the fourth or fifth time and shut the door upon the last comers, when we met in the little front entry. Mrs. Todd was not in a bad temper, but highly amused. 'I've been havin' all sorts o' social privileges, you may have observed. They didn't seem to consider that if they could only hold out till afternoon they'd know as much as I did. There wa'n't but one o' the whole sixteen that showed real interest, the rest demeaned themselves to ask out o' cheap curiosity; no, there wa'n't but one showed any real feelin'.'

'Miss Maria Harris, you mean?' and Mrs. Todd laughed.

'Certain, dear,' she agreed, 'how you do understand poor human natur'!'

A short distance down the hilly street stood a narrow house that was newly painted white. It blinded one's eyes to catch the reflection of the sun. It was the house of the minister, and a waggon had just stopped before it; a man was helping a woman to alight, and they stood side by side for a moment, while Johnny Bowden appeared as if by magic, and climbed to the waggon-seat. Then they went into the house and shut the door. Mrs. Todd and I stood close together and watched; the tears were running down her cheeks. I watched Johnny Bowden, who made light of so great a moment by so handling the whip that the old white Caplin horse started up from time to time and was inexorably stopped as if he had some idea of running away. There was something in the back of the waggon which now and then claimed the boy's attention; he leaned over as if there were something very precious left in his charge; perhaps it was only Esther's little trunk going to its new home.

At last the door of the parsonage opened, and two figures came out. The minister followed them and stood in the doorway, delaying them with parting words; he could not have thought it was a time for admonition.

'He's all alone; his wife's up to Portland to her sister's,' said Mrs. Todd aloud, in a matter-of-fact voice. 'She's a nice woman, but she might ha' talked too much. There! see, they're comin' here. I didn't know how 't would be. Yes, they're comin' up to see us before they go home. I declare, if William ain't lookin' just like a king!'

Mrs. Todd took one step forward, and we stood and waited. The happy pair came walking up the street, Johnny Bowden driving ahead. I heard a plaintive little cry from time to time to which in the excitement of the moment I had not stopped to listen; but when William and Esther had come and shaken hands with Mrs. Todd and then with me, all in silence, Esther stepped quickly to the back of the waggon, and unfastening some cords returned to us carrying a little white lamb. She gave a shy glance at William as she fondled it and held it to her heart, and then, still silent, we went into the house together. The lamb had stopped bleating. It was lovely to see Esther carry it in her arms.

When we got into the house, all the repression of Mrs. Todd's usual manner was swept away by her flood of feeling. She took Esther's thin figure, lamb and all, to her heart and held her there, kissing her as she might have kissed a child, and then held out her hand to William and they gave each other the kiss of peace. This was so moving, so tender, so free from their usual fetter of self-consciousness, that Esther and I could not help giving each other a happy glance of comprehension. I never saw a young bride half so touching in her happiness as Esther was that day of her wedding. We took the cake and wine of the marriage feast together, always in silence, like a true sacrament, and then to my astonishment I found that sympathy and public interest in so great an occasion were going to have their way. I shrank from the thought of William's possible sufferings, but he welcomed both the first group of neighbours and the last with heartiness; and when at last they had gone, for there were thought-less loiterers in Dunnet Landing, I made ready with eager zeal and walked with William and Esther to the water-side. It was only a little way, and kind faces nodded reassuringly from the windows, while kind voices spoke from the doors. Esther carried the lamb on one arm; she had found time to tell me that its mother had died that morning and she could not bring herself to the thought of leaving it behind. She kept the other hand on William's arm until we reached the landing. Then he shook hands with me, and looked me full in the face to be sure I understood how happy he was, and stepping into the boat held out his arms to Esther – at last she was his own.

I watched him make a nest for the lamb out of an old sea-cloak at Esther's feet, and then he wrapped her own shawl round her shoulders, and finding a pin in the lapel of his Sunday coat he pinned it for her. She looked at him fondly while he did this, and then glanced up at us, a pretty, girlish colour brightening her cheeks.

We stood there together and watched them go far out into the bay. The sunshine of the May day was low now, but there was a steady breeze, and the boat moved well.

'Mother'll be watching for them,' said Mrs. Todd. 'Yes, mother'll be watching all day, and waiting. She'll be so happy to have Esther come.'

We went home together up the hill, and Mrs. Todd said nothing more; but we held each other's hands all the way.

CHAPTER TWENTY-FOUR

The Backward View

*

At last it was the time of late summer, when the house was cool and damp in the morning, and all the light seemed to come through green leaves; but at the first step out of doors the sunshine always laid a warm hand on my shoulder, and the clear, high sky seemed to lift quickly as I looked at it. There was no autumnal mist on the coast, nor any August fog; instead of these, the sea, the sky, all the long shore line and the inland hills, with every bush of bay and every fir-top, gained a deeper colour and a sharper clearness. There was something shining in the air, and a kind of lustre on the water and the pasture grass,— a northern look that, except at this moment of the year, one must go far to seek. The sunshine of a northern summer was coming to its lovely end.

The days were few then at Dunnet Landing, and I let each of them slip away unwillingly as a miser spends his coins. I wished to have one of my first weeks back again, with those long hours when nothing happened except the growth of herbs and the course of the sun. Once I had not even known where to go for a walk; now there were many delightful things to be done and done again, as if I were in London. I felt hurried and full of pleasant engagements, and the days flew by like a handful of flowers flung to the sea wind.

THE BACKWARD VIEW

At last I had to say good-bye to all my Dunnet Landing friends, and my homelike place in the little house, and return to the world in which I feared to find myself a foreigner. There may be restrictions to such a summer's happiness, but the ease that belongs to simplicity is charming enough to make up for whatever a simple life may lack, and the gifts of peace are not for those who live in the thick of battle.

I was to take the small unpunctual steamer that went down the bay in the afternoon, and I sat for a while by my window looking out on the green herb garden, with regret for company. Mrs. Todd had hardly spoken all day except in the briefest and most disapproving way; it was as if we were on the edge of a quarrel. It seemed impossible to take my departure with anything like composure. At last I heard a footstep, and looked up to find that Mrs. Todd was standing at the door.

'I've seen to everything now,' she told me in an unusually loud and business-like voice. 'Your trunks are on the w'arf by this time. Cap'n Bowden he come and took 'em down himself, an' is going to see that they're safe aboard. Yes, I've seen to all your 'rangements,' she repeated in a gentler tone. 'These things I've left on the kitchen table you'll want to carry by hand; the basket needn't be returned. I guess I shall walk over toward the Port now an' inquire how old Mis' Edward Caplin is.'

I glanced at my friend's face, and saw a look that touched me to the heart. I had been sorry enough before to go away.

'I guess you'll excuse me if I ain't down there to stand round on the w'arf and see you go,' she said, still trying to be gruff. 'Yes, I ought to go over and inquire for Mis' Edward Caplin; it's her third shock, and if mother gets in on Sunday she'll want to know just how the old lady is.' With this last word Mrs. Todd turned and left me as if with sudden thought of something she had forgotten, so that I felt sure she was coming back, but presently I heard her go out of the kitchen door and walk down the path toward the gate. I could not part so; I ran after her to say good-bye, but she shook her head and waved her hand without looking back when she heard my hurrying steps, and so went away down the street.

When I went in again the little house had suddenly grown lonely, and my room looked empty as it had the day I came. I and all my belongings had died out of it, and I knew how it would seem when Mrs. Todd came back and found her lodger gone. So we die before our own eyes; so we see some chapters of our lives come to their natural end.

I found the little packages on the kitchen table. There was a quaint West Indian basket which I knew its owner had valued, and which I had once admired; there was an affecting provision laid beside it for my seafaring supper, with a neatly tied bunch of southernwood and a twig of bay, and a little old leather box which held the coral pin that Nathan Todd brought home to give to poor Joanna.

There was still an hour to wait, and I went up to the hill just above the schoolhouse and sat there thinking of things, and looking off to sea, and watching for the boat to come in sight. I could see Green Island, small and darkly wooded at that distance; below me were the houses of the village with their apple-trees and bits of garden ground. Presently, as I looked at the pastures beyond, I caught a last glimpse of Mrs. Todd herself, walking slowly in the footpath that led along, following the shore toward the Port. At such a distance one can feel the large, positive qualities that control a character. Close at hand, Mrs. Todd seemed able and warm-hearted and quite absorbed in her bustling industries, but her distant figure looked mateless and appealing, with something about it that was strangely self-pos-sessed and mysterious. Now and then she stooped to pick something, – it might have been her favourite pennyroyal, – and at last I lost sight of her as she slowly crossed an open space on one of the higher points of land, and disappeared again behind a dark clump of juniper and the pointed firs.

As I came away on the little coastwise steamer, there was an old sea running which made the surf leap high on all the rocky shores. I stood on deck, looking back, and watched the busy gulls agree and turn, and sway together down the long slopes of air, then separate hastily and plunge into the waves. The tide was setting in, and plenty of small fish were coming with it, unconscious of the silver flashing of the great birds overhead and the quickness of their fierce beaks. The sea was full of life and spirit, the tops of the waves flew back as if they were winged like the gulls themselves, and like them had the freedom of the wind. Out in the main channel we passed a bent-shouldered old fisherman bound for the evening round among his lobster traps. He was toiling along with short oars, and the dory tossed and sank and tossed again with the steamer's waves. I saw that it was old Elijah Tilley, and though we had so long been strangers we had come to be warm friends, and I wished that he had waited for one of his mates, it was such hard work to row along shore through rough seas and tend the traps alone. As we passed I waved my hand and tried to call to him, and he looked up and answered my farewells by a solemn nod. The little town, with the tall masts of its disabled schooners in the inner bay, stood high above the flat sea for a few minutes, then it sank back into the uniformity of the the coast, and became indistinguishable from the other towns that looked as if they were crumbled on the furzy-green stoniness of the shore.

The small outer islands of the bay were covered among the ledges with turf that looked as fresh as the early grass; there had been some days of rain the week before, and the darker green of the sweet-fern was

252

scattered on all the pasture heights. It looked like the beginning of summer ashore, though the sheep, round and warm in their winter wool, betrayed the season of the year as they went feeding along the slopes in the low afternoon sunshine. Presently the wind began to blow, and we struck out seaward to double the long sheltering headland of the cape, and when I looked back again, the islands and the headland had run together and Dunnet Landing and all its coasts were lost to sight.